STEPHEN E. AMBROSE

THIS VAST LAND

A Young Man's Journal of the Lewis and Clark Expedition

A Novel

Simon & Schuster Books for Young Readers

New York   London   Toronto   Sydney   Singapore

SIMON & SCHUSTER BOOKS FOR YOUNG READERS

An imprint of Simon & Schuster Children's Publishing Division

1230 Avenue of the Americas, New York, New York 10020

This work of fiction is based on the journals of Meriwether Lewis, William Clark, the men of the expedition, and the imagination of the author. Descriptions and dialogue from the journals are mixed in throughout it.

This book is a work of fiction. Any references to historical events, real people, or real locales are used fictitiously. Other names, characters, places, and incidents are products of the author's imagination, and any resemblance to actual events or locales or persons, living or dead, is entirely coincidental.

Copyright © 2003 by Ambrose & Ambrose, Inc.

All rights reserved, including the right of reproduction in whole or in part in any form.

SIMON & SCHUSTER BOOKS FOR YOUNG READERS is a trademark of Simon & Schuster.

Book design by O'Lanso Gabbidon

The text for this book is set in Berkeley.

Manufactured in the United States of America

10 9 8 7 6 5 4 3 2 1

CIP data for this book is available from the Library of Congress.

ISBN 0-689-86448-5

FIRST F EDITION

This book is dedicated to all youngsters
who follow the trail with their family.
Happy trails.

FOREWORD

In the spring of 2002 my father finished writing his last nonfiction book, *To America*. Its completion had been very important to him. Then, as summer came on, his illness began to take its toll on him. Seeing him struggle was hard on all of his family. As ever, he took great joy in being with us and in researching and writing. With *To America* completed, though, all of us worried. He had always been driven to write, to create, and now there was no goal in sight. There was just the illness to fight.

One afternoon he told my mother and me that he wanted to write a novel, just for the fun of it.

"Like the one about George Shannon you wrote back in Berkeley?" I asked.

"Exactly!" he exclaimed, then sighed. "That's long lost, for sure."

My mother smiled. "No, Steve, I have it here somewhere."

He brightened, pronounced every syllable of "wonderful," and looked at us expectantly. Before too long Mom went to see if she could find it.

My father spent the last few weeks of his life happily editing this manuscript. It came straight from his heart. His own boyish enthusiasm for life and adventure, his love of being part of a team, fill every page. He poured all of his knowledge of the men and their expedition into it, but he also took liberties with the story as he saw fit. We were happy that he had another challenge ahead of him and enjoyed the time we had with him. My parents' friend in the Bay, Tammy Cimalore, gave her time generously to my folks during these dark days. We are all so grateful to her for her help, her kindness, her friendship.

Months after he left us I began work on getting it published, just as he had wanted. The process of editing the manuscript, without him around to guard his vision, was difficult. My mother, always his first editor, guided it. My eldest sister, Stephanie, a Lewis and Clark scholar in her own right, gave the manuscript a careful examination and made some valuable edits. To be fair to her, though, whenever there was a tough choice between "historical accuracy" and "artistic license," I left his work the way he wrote it. My sister Grace, and brothers Andy and Barry, as well as our cousin Edie read the manuscript and helped. Reading it, for us, was bittersweet. We can all hear him so clearly.

Hugh Ambrose
New Orleans
May 2003

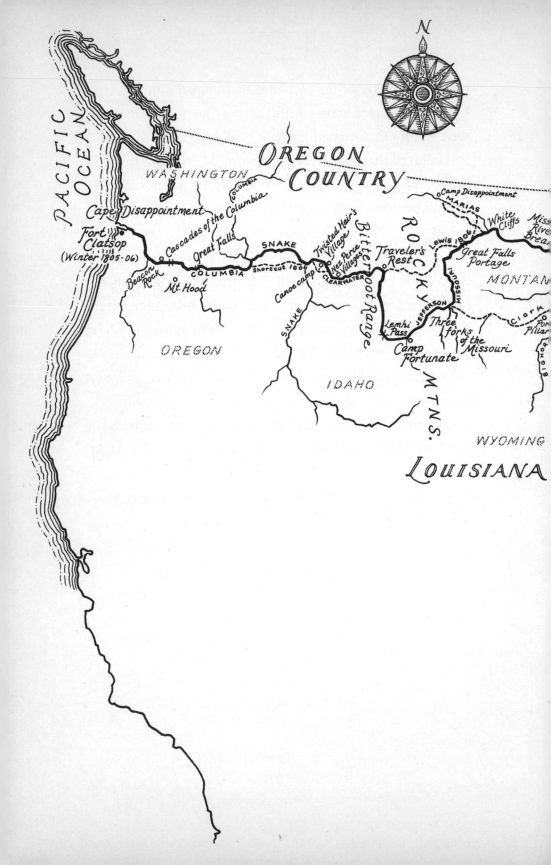

Lewis and Clark Expedition

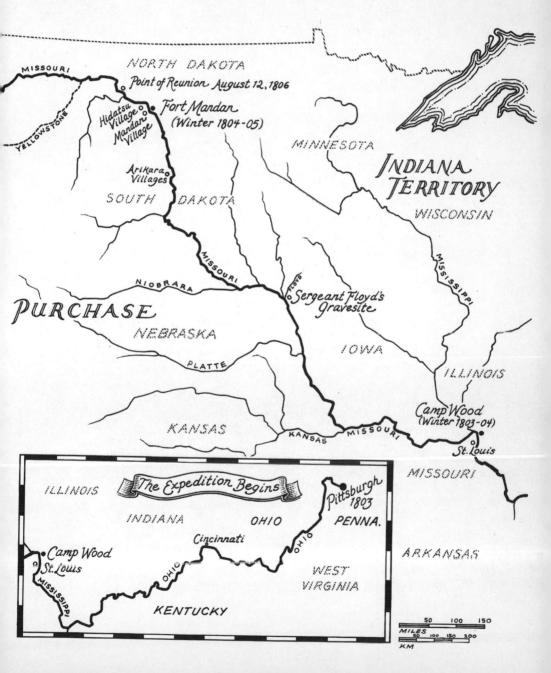

MISSOURI

NORTH DAKOTA

Point of Reunion August 12, 1806

Hidatsu Village
Mandan Village

Fort Mandan (Winter 1804-05)

YELLOWSTONE

MINNESOTA

INDIANA TERRITORY

WISCONSIN

Arikara Villages

SOUTH DAKOTA

MISSOURI

MISSISSIPPI

NIOBRARA

PURCHASE

NEBRASKA

FLOYD

Sergeant Floyd's Gravesite

IOWA

ILLINOIS

PLATTE

Camp Wood (Winter 1803-04)

KANSAS

KANSAS

MISSOURI

St. Louis

MISSOURI

The Expedition Begins

ILLINOIS

INDIANA

OHIO

Pittsburgh 1803

PENNA.

Cincinnati

OHIO

Camp Wood
St. Louis

MISSISSIPPI

OHIO

WEST VIRGINIA

ARKANSAS

KENTUCKY

50   100   150
MILES
50 100 150 200
KM

PITTSBURGH TO WOOD RIVER

Aug. 30, 1803.

This day Capt. Lewis said I could accompany him and his party on their trip to St. Louis and then up the Missouri River. It has taken me six weeks to persuade him, ever since July when I walked many miles to get to Pittsburgh.

When I introduced myself to Capt. Lewis he looked to me to be a decent honorable man. Taller and thinner than most men, he had a distinguished face, was clean shaven and clear-eyed, with a prominent nose, a fixed chin, and a determined mouth. I judged him to be a fair man and did not hesitate to tell him I wanted to join his Expedition.

He pretended he did not know what I was referring to, he tried to brush me aside, he said he was an army officer on a recruiter's mission only and that I was too young for the Army. I protested that I'd be having my 18th birthday soon and informed him that it was no use pretending, every soul in Ohio and Kentucky knew that he was gathering a Party for an Expedition to go Overland to the Pacific Ocean. There is the greatest excitement at the rumors and the prospect of this Great Adventure. It was like an opportunity to sail with Columbus. He was going to have lots of Volunteers and I just wanted him to remember that I was First.

I told him I would make a good soldier. He said I was too soft. I said I would make a good hunter and woodsman. He said I was too citified. I told him it was not my fault I grew up in Pennsylvania that I would learn the ways of the wilderness. He said there would not be time to teach. I said he would never find a man more eager. He said eagerness was more often a hurt than a help. Besides he would be able to select his crew from the best young men on the frontier, so what should he take me when he could have the best.

I am extremely well read, I replied.

No one is going to have time to be discussing books

around the campfire, he said. It left me in despair. He said he thought I would go far in life, but not with him. Not on this Expedition. I was too young, too green. Perhaps next time when I was a bit older.

Oh Captain! Captain! I cried out. There never can be a next time. There is only one time to be the first across the Continent.

He said No and turned on his heel. But two river men told him that the Ohio was too low, that he would never get down it until spring. I seized my chance to tell Capt. Lewis that I can swim and can stick with it all day. He was in need of trusty men to get this great bulk of a keel boat over the riffels and sandbars and rapids, men who aren't afraid to jump over and grasp a line and tussle with the current and the debris and the Boat. I am one of those men! I said. He grunted, Come on Aboard. We leave in the morning. I run off to my lodging to gather up my blanket roll. I am going west!

When I returned he handed me this book, bound in Leather and folio sized. That, he said, is your journal. I want you to write every day's happenings, as you will see things I don't, and I want as full a record of this Expedition as could be.

Aug. 31, '03.

We set off this day and made only four miles and I am too tired to write.

Sept. 1, '03.

Twelve miles today. My wrists and arms are sore.

Sept. 9, '03.

Wheeling, Ohio. It has taken us more than a week to come from Pittsburgh to here, as a consequence of the water being sometimes only six inches deep.

I have pulled and pushed and paddled and plunged into the water twenty times a day, and three or four times a day I have had to struggle to shore, find the nearest farmer, hire his team of Ox, accompany him back to the River, hook up the Ox, and pull the Boat thru a sandbar. No slave ever worked as I have, never have I been so sore in all my Joins. My feet are cut and bruised from snags and rocks, my skin is so burned I look like a Red Indian, but my heart has Joy in it, because of the last part, seeing the Boat about to go broadside on a rock, I averted the danger by pushing with my pole and Capt. Lewis noticed and called out, Good Work, George!

Sept. 13, '03.
Made twenty miles to day and arrived this evening in the village of Marietta, Ohio. Capt. Lewis told me as I was too young to drink corn liquor I would stand watch over the Boat tonight when the rest of the Crew was free to go into the Village.

Sept. 20, '03.
Low water is a plague, but Capt. Lewis declares that it shall not prevent our proceeding, that he is determined to get forward though we should not be able to make more than a mile a day. He informs the crew that we shall move on even should we not be able to make greater speed than a boat's length per day!

Sept. 25, '03.
Good progress this day. Capt. Lewis dismissed two more men for insubordination. One had shouted at him to cook his own damn food, the other cried out, Do it

yourself Damn you, when Capt. Lewis told him to lash the boat to the wharf. I think they wanted to go anyhow. Another man deserted last night. The work is too hard. We are down to six.

Sept. 26, '03.

Last night Capt. Lewis took on a new man whose name is John Colter and who is only two years older than me. He did not have to be very persuasive as we are so short on crew just at this time. Colter heard about this Expedition in Staunton, Virginia, and set off immediately to find us and sign up. He has been hunting all his life and promises to show me how. He is as eager as me to get to the Pacific Ocean. He expects honor and glory, but the magnet for him was just seeing all that new country that he says has never before been seen by a white man. We talked far into the night about how far it stretches and what the mountains might be like and the Indians we will meet and etc. His excitement at the Prospect makes my own grow.

Sept. 29, '03.

Colter challenged me to a race this morning he won easily. We wrestled, he threw me even though I outweigh him by 20 lbs. He cannot read or write. What is the use of that, he asks. He intends to spend his life in the Wild. I find I envy him and wish I had his skills rather than the ones I have which are useless in the Wild.

Oct. 1, '03.

Last night Colter and some of the other men asked me if I wished to go into Cincinnati with them to find some whores at the taverns. I said no that I did not drink and I did not go whoring. Colter called me a Baby. I replied that Capt. Lewis had warned me about the whores and the venereal disease and crabs and that he had told me that I should hold myself Pure and in Readiness for my wedding night, and that was what he was doing and I should do the same.

Oct. 15, '03.

We arrived this evening in Clarksville, Indiana Territory, across the river from Louisville, Kentucky. When we tied up,

Capt. Lewis took me for his meeting with the Clark brothers—General George Rogers Clark, the hero of the War for Independence, and his younger brother Capt. William Clark, who is to join our Expedition as co-commander.

General Clark is 18 years older than his brother who resembles him in his strength and height except that Captain Clark has red hair, the General's hair is grey. Capt. Clark is big in his shoulders, rugged in his face, tall and muscular in his arms and legs, capable of doing almost anything or so he appears to me.

I asked Gen'l Clark did he think the Federalists were right, that we would find Louisiana a desert. No, he said, I anticipate a land as green as Ohio. He damned the Feds as obnoxious pettifogging bastards whose only thought was to stop settlement in the West. Capts. Clark and Lewis heartily agreed, they thought the whole of the Continent, not just Louisiana, should be a part of the U. States and that by God if they had anything to do with it, it would.

Go for it, Boys, Gen'l Clark said, go for it. His eyes lit as he spoke, he had thunder in his voice, it made me realize what a great man he is, it was a thrill to hear him. I would follow the man anywhere, no wonder he took Vincennes.

One other man joins us here, as a servant not a

soldier, he is Capt. Clark's slave York, a huge tall man, taller than Capt. C. himself, very big in the shoulders, black as the darkest night. I do not much care for slavery or for black men.

Oct. 19, '03.

Colter is instructing me how to shoot and I have finally mastered the intricate process of loading and preparing my piece to fire. I can pour in the powder, tamp down the wadding, ran home my bullet, prepare my flintlock, find a good rest for my rifle, take and hold a deep breath and squeeze the trigger. Today I got a shot at a squirrel which I hit and which I roasted and ate tonight.

Oct. 20, '03.

I killed my first deer today, it was fit and fine. I shot it clean through its lungs, it took two jumps and fell. Colter anointed me with the deer's blood, smearing it on my forehead, he says this is always done for a man's first deer.

Oct. 21, '03.

The Capts. held a ceremony today inducting sixteen of us into the Corps of Discovery. Capt. Clark swore us in, in a most solemn manner. He said we were all hand-picked, that for each man selected he had turned down ten other volunteers, because this Expedition needed the biggest, the bravest, the boldest and the best young men that old Kentucky and Virginia, Indiana and Ohio had to offer and we were them. He marched in front of us, telling us that he would make us into real soldiers, not any damned militia outfit. His talk was hot and spurts of dust sprang at his heels.

Capt. Lewis next addressed us. Pointing west, down river, he said that out there lives our destiny. A great unknown empire beyond the Mississippi, the last great unknown empire on this earth. It would be our privilege to explore it and report on what we find and secure Title to it. Exploring the West has been the darling object of my life, he said, and now we are to do it together. We will blaze the way.

Nov. 11, '03.

We arrived at Fort Massac in Illinois Territory at noon today. A number of volunteers were eager to join our party, but the Capts. accepted only two of them, Joseph Whitehouse and John Newman.

One man Capt. Lewis hired as a civilian interpreter and hunter, George Drewyer, a French-Canadian-Indian. He is a small man, quiet and dark-skinned who is skilled in the way of the wilderness and the Indians. He can speak their languages or converse with them through signs.

Nov. 14, '03.

We have reached the discharge of the Ohio into the Mississippi. Capt. Lewis and me are the only ones to come the whole route from Pittsburgh. The Mississippi is broad, swift and turbulent. Drewyer says the Shawnee Indians call it the Father of Waters.

Nov. 17, '03.

We spent the past three days measuring the rivers and making celestial observations. Newman, Colter, Whitehouse, York, and me paddle Capt. C. around in a pirogue while he runs Cords to measure width and tops weighted lines to measure depth. Capt. Lewis uses the sextant.

Dec. 13, '03.

This day we arrive at Camp Wood, on the Illinois side, 17-1/2 miles above St. Louis, directly across from the discharge of the Missouri River at which we get out for a first look. She is a proud and powerful river. She is strong enough to force her brown muddy water across the Mississippi, this drives the blue water of the Mississippi into a narrow channel on the East bank. The Missouri carries a tremendous quantity of logs, stumps, roots, whole trees along with her which pile up on this beach.

Dec. 25, '03.

This is my first Christmas away from my family.

I gave Colter a pair of leggings I made from deer hide, he gives me a pair of mittens from a bear. But our best Present was the finishing of our Log Huts which we move into tonight, they will serve admirable. This morning we went out hunting for turkeys and by noon had ten prime gobblers roasting over the fire. The men sang and danced to the fiddle, they purchased whiskey from peddlers out of Cahokia, the ardent spirits made them merry.

WINTER AT WOOD RIVER

Jan'y 2, '04.

We commence building lockers for the Boat under the direction of Gass, our carpenter, also adding benches for the oarsmen.

Jan'y 21, '04.

We pack and unpack goods all the day long. We pack lanterns and lamps and candles and pots and pan and brass kettles, chisels and adze and saws and ax and hammers and nails and needles and awls and spoons and augers and ink and paper and whiskey barrels and tea and coffee and sacks of flour and sugar, and much more.

Jan'y 28, '04.

Last night with the Capts. gone to St. Louis to purchase more provisions, I had my first whiskey. Colter gave it to me, he said one little sip cannot Hurt. I took it, it burned my throat. I run to the river and crank down near a gallon of water. Colter laughed at me.

Some time later I felt a warm glow run through my body and felt relaxed and Peaceful and Eager all at once. I decided to take only one more little Sip, which could not hurt. Colter took the jug from Rubin Fields and handed it to me; I tilted and swallowed and it burned again but not so bad this time. By 12 o'clock me and Colter and the Fields brothers were sitting on the bank tilting the jug and singing Little Brown Jug.

The Moon was full and the Missouri shined in its light, pushing against the Mississippi. Colter shook his clenched fist at the Missouri and called out to her that we are coming you Big Son of a Bitch, we are coming. Joseph Fields called out, We are not afraid of you Missouri, by God we are not afraid.

☙

March 3, '04.

Today I helped Gass attach the swivel gun to the deck of the boat. The lockers are all in place, they open in such a way as to provide instant Breastworks strong enough to turn back arrows. These breastworks plus the swivel gun make the Boat into a floating Fortress.

March 6, '04.

Newman bought a keg of whiskey from one of the local peddlers last night so the Fields brothers, Colter, Silas Goodrich, Newman and Shields and me went to our stop on the bank to drink it after we suppered. We again informed the Missouri that we are coming, she had best look smart and the Indians, too.

When the keg ran dry we stumbled our way back to our boats. Newman fell outside the Capts.' Hut. Capt. C. called out to Keep the Peace. Newman shouted back to him to keep his own damn peace, which was an error on his part.

This morning Capt. C. confined us all to quarters after work detail. Newman got fifty lashes for insubordination. Sgt. Ordway lays those lashes on very precisely with his whip, making certain that cuts and welts cover Newman's entire back.

March 19, '04.

Yesterday Drewyer showed me how to persuade a running deer to stop in his tracks. Today Capt. C. sent me and Colter out to hunt. A buck broke from some brush in front of us and dashed through to a clearing. Colter was cursing as he failed to have his cat-o'-nine-tails and could not shoot.

I gave a long loud whistle as Drewyer had taught me, the deer stopped, threw his legs wide, held his tail and head high, his big ears quivering to locate the source of the whistle. I primed my rifle, aimed, fired, and dropped the Buck.

Well I will be damned, said Colter. Where did you learn that trick?

Drewyer, I replied.

Ain't he something, Colter said. He is teaching me how to talk to the Turkeys, that man I swear can talk a tom right up to his feet and get him to hop aboard if he wants.

April 1, '04.

Today the Capts. posted a Notice to the Detachment, that they had selected those who were going on the

Permanent Detachment all the way to the Pacific Ocean and back. The rest would turn tack at our winter quarters, when the ice breaks up on the river, and go to St. Louis to deliver mail, specimens, reports & etc. I was listed as a member of the Permanent Detachment. This is the grandest achievement of my life to date.

The Order went on to divide us into three squads, each commanded by one of the Sgts., Pryor, Floyd, and Ordway. I am to be in Sgt. Pryor's squad along with Shields and Joe Whitehouse and five others. I then read further down the order and read this: "During indisposition of Sgt. Pryor (who is sick), George Shannon is appointed (pretempor) to discharge his the Said Pryor's duty in his squad.

In short, I am in charge until Pryor recovers, this is a Singular Honor. If only my family could see me now, a squad leader in the Corps of Discovery!

May 6, '04.

Several of the Country people come to camp to challenge me to a shooting contest. All the settlers get beat and lose their best. I won a gallon of milk which I share with my teacher Drewyer. This is the first bet I've ever won shooting. Drewyer says I am near ready for the Wilderness.

May 23, '04.

Completed loading the pirogues, all in readiness to depart. My muscles are the strongest they have yet been, I am ready to meet the challenge of this mighty Missouri River. We all of us have confidence in our Captains.

TO THE MOUTH OF THE KANSAS

May 14, '04.

At four o'clock we raise the sail in a gentle breeze and bend our oars. We have 22 men of the Permanent Detachment at the oars, the Boat fairly flies. Two pirogues comprise the balance of our fleet, one the red pirogue, contains the seven Engagees, the other the white pirogue contains Corp. Warfington and five soldiers who are to accompany to our winter quarters and return to boat to St. Louis in the spring.

We pulled across the Mississippi and into the Missouri to commence our Adventure. Sgt. Ordway amidships calls out a count we stroke in rhythm, there is a sense of power as we stroke together. We make four miles and come to an island where we make camp.

May 16, '04.

We pulled to at the landing in St. Charles on the right hand bank at noon. This village has 100 homes, these people are French they appear Poor and polite.

May 17, '04.

Last night Wm. Werner, Hugh Hall, and John Collins sneaked out of camp and went to a ball in St. Charles, when they returned about midnight I was on Guard. I challenged them, they replied, Go to Hell, and made a ruckus. This morning Capt. C. brought a Court Martial with Sgt. Ordway in charge. Each man was found guilty of absent without leave, but only Collins got 50 lashes.

May 18, '04.

Capt. C. enlisted two new men for the Permanent Detachment, they are Frenchies. Privates Cruzzate and Labiche. Cruzzate is said to be the best Boatman on the Missouri, he will take his place in the bow to watch for obstructions and provide guidance. He is half Indian as is Labiche, both men have been far up this river, Labiche so far as the Mandans.

May 23, '04.

Yesterday we made 19 miles, today nine. We came to early today, a result of Capt. C. wishing to pay his Respects to Mr. Daniel Boone, the man who opened Kentucky. Colter and me expressed our wish to Shake the Hands of the Old Hero, we were allowed to join the Capts. We stepped along over a fair rode to Mr. Boone's cabin in a clearing in the woods near the Femme Osage River. He is a short man near 70 years of age, his face wrinkled. He informs us he can still plow and hunt and wanted for but little, his only fear is getting hemmed in again as happened to him back in Kentucky. He thought this move to the Missouri country would be his last wilderness move, that he was tired of having to outrun settlers.

He introduced his wife, children, and grandchildren. He showed us his fertile farm with cattle. His land grant comes from the Spaniards, but he is pleased to be in the

U. States territory again. His cabin consists of three floors including a loft. It is ingenious, the shutters close from within, there are rifle niches scattered throughout, in short he can instantly convert her into a fortress. He stores his silver on the second floor because he explains Indians will not climb to a second floor. He keeps sufficient goods in his root cellar to sustain an Indian siege for a month. He built a school for his grandchildren.

The Capts. informed him of our purpose. He expressed his approval and his Satisfaction at the number of Kentucky boys in the Permanent Detachment. He thought Kentucky boys can see us through. He slapped his knee, exclaiming by Thunder he Wished to God he was Young enough to accompany the Corps of Discovery.

There was nothing like being the first to see a place, he said. He explained that when he first crossed the Cumberland Gap and looked down on Kentucky he thought it was too beautiful to bear, that his Heart would burst for the very joy of it.

I expressed the Desire to carry something of Daniel Boone across the Rocky Mountains to the Ocean. Mr.

Boone was much pleased, he gave me a knife which he had with him when he crossed the Cumberland Gap. He said it had saved his life many a time and would mine and that I should guard it with my life.

May 25, '04.

This day we arrive at La Charrette, a village of seven houses, the people poor. They give us eggs and milk. This is a beautiful country, hardwoods abound, the land is Fertile and well watered. Capt. Lewis calls it as good a farming country as can be, Capt. C. remarks that it will soon be fully settled.

June 16, '04.

This morning I accompany Drewyer on a hunt. We climbed to the Prairie, this is a beautiful rolling country, herds of deer at every waterhole, they feed on the young willow.

At noon Drewyer discovered a colt which was in all probability escaped from an Osage War Party. He approached it slowly calling out Indian words softly, he had made a halter out of his rope belt. He rubbed the nose of the Colt then slipped over the Halter and thus procured himself a means for hauling meat easier than his shoulders.

June 26, '04.

Today we came to the mouth of the Kansas River. We make camp in the point between the two rivers. Here Capt. C. announced we will delay three or four days to make observations and to rest.

June 27, '04.

The Capts. make celestial observations. We repair the red pirogue, clean out the Boat and sun our powder and woolen articles. The Kansas carries vast quantities of sand. The waters of this river taste very disagreeable.

TO THE SIOUX NATION

July 4, '04.

At dawn the Capts. order us to fire off the bow gun to celebrate our nation's 28th birthday—which makes it ten years older than me. Capt. C. names the creek on which we camp tonight Independence Creek. We fire the bow piece again and the Capts. issue two gills of whiskey. It is a proud thing to penetrate the rich, untapped land of Louisiana.

July 20, '04.

Capt. C. observed today that our Party is much healthier on this Voyage than Parties of the same number have been in any other situation. If so, we say, we should like to see the other Parties. Boils, tumors, head aches, sun burn, and sore eyes from the sun on the water all day, bad backs, these are the characteristics of the Corps of Discovery on this accursed river.

We pass abandoned Indian villages. Cruzzate, who wintered here one Winter with the Otos, gives us as the reason for their being abandoned the Smallpox which swept through here some years ago. It reduced the Otos from 700 to 300 lodges in a year. Labiche reckons it was worse among the Mahars.

July 21, '04.

An early start, at noon we passed the discharge of the great River Platte. We are now 600 miles and 68 days from Camp Wood, or one half of the way to the Mandans.

The Platte is a horrid river, shallow, swift, strong enough to force herself across the Missouri, she carries tons of sand which piles up on the opposite bank. She cannot be ascended any distance even in a pirogue due to her great velocity and width and lack of depth. Her channel, Cruzzate says, is near impossible to find.

I fell this day and lost Mr. Boone's knife and looked up and saw a rattlesnake shaking his tail, with his face just in front of my face, his teeth bared. Moses Reed who was with me called out, Hang on George, and retrieved the knife. Just as the snake was commencing to strike Reed with a quick stroke cut off his head.

We roasted the rattler and after eating we talked. Reed says he has had enough of this life, that it is too much work and not enough play, he wants to desert and live with the Indians the way the Frenchies do. I told him he was a fool that he will be disgraced if he deserts, he replies what does he care what the world thinks of him, he wants to be happy now and can be here living the good life.

I reminded him that he took a solemn Oath, that his was a Duty to the Capts., to the members of the Corps of Discovery, to his country, but he merely laughs and says he is going at the first opportunity. He seeks my aid in deserting. I reply never. Says as I now owe him my life I am honor bound to help him to discharge my debt. I scarcely know what to do, I am in a quandary.

Aug. 3, '04.

Some Chiefs from the Oto Nation came to camp. The Capts. talked with them through Labiche. Capt. Lewis gave the principal speech, he informed the Chiefs that they had a new father, the Pres. of the U. States, Mr. Thomas Jefferson, and that the new father was anxious to learn all he could about his children the Oto so that he could best help them and protect them. He would be well pleased if they made a peace with all Nations, that they should be men of their word.

The Chiefs replied. They promised to be good Children to their new Father, they wondered did their new Father have any presents for them. Their last new Father, the Spaniard, gave them presents. The Capts. gave them a flag of the U. States, one of the small medals each for the Chiefs, a bottle of whiskey for the warriors who were soon drunk and commenced whooping, hollering, dancing & etc. They became insensible.

During the party Reed took Mr. Boone's knife from me.

Aug. 4, '04.

A hot day. Set out early, pulled six miles. When we come to at 12 o'clock Reed recollected that he had left his knife in the camp of last night. Capt. C. said to forget it as we have plenty of knives, but when Reed said it is Mr. Boone's knife borrowed from me, Capt. Lewis asked me, Is this true? My head was spinning, I could not trust myself to speak, I nodded only. Capt. Lewis told Reed to go back and get it and not make such a mistake again.

Aug. 9, '04.

Drewyer and some others have been hunting for Reed for four days, with orders to shoot him if necessary, but to bring him back. I am frightened to think of the matter. We made 16 miles yesterday, 17 and 1/2 today. The river contains immense numbers of Pelicans which are a large white bird that fishes, they are awkward on land but expert flyers. When we disturb them they soar to great heights, they fly like eagles, it is a grand site when they wheel into the sun and flash against the blue sky. I wish I was an artist, these are scenes I shall never forget but can never describe adequately. Sometimes the sky is white with them. Capt. C. thinks there are 4,000 of them, Capt. Lewis reckons 5,000.

Aug. 17, '04.

This evening Drewyer returned. He had Reed who looked miserable as well he might. We proceeded to the Trial of Reed, charged with Desertion. He confessed that he had deserted and stole a public rifle, shot pouch, powder and ball and asked the Capts. to be as lenient with him as the situation allowed. They sentenced him to run the gauntlet four times and issued each of us a staunch willow stick. All laid on with a will to let Reed know what they think of deserters.

The Oto Chiefs who are with us protested this whipping. Capt. Lewis explained to them the necessity of it. They admitted the need for Example but in their country they killed a man to show the Example, no one, not even a child was ever whipped. These Chiefs cried when we whipped Reed.

Reed is no longer a member of the Permanent

Detachment although he will continue to pull an ore. He will be sent back to St. Louis in the Spring. In the meanwhile no one is to speak to him.

This day is Capt. Lewis's 30th Birthday which fact seems to set him back, we celebrated anyway with an extra gill of whisky each and Cruzzate brought out his Fiddle, we danced.

Sgt. Floyd is sick these past few days, he complains of a fierce pain in his belly. Capt. Lewis gives him some of Rush's pills, a purgative the captains regard as sovereign for all illness.

Aug. 20, '04.

Sgt. Floyd died after part of the day. We laid out his body as well as possible under the circumstances and carried him to the top of a bluff where we buried him with full military honors and ceremony, we fire a volley & etc. Capt. C. spoke over his gravesite. This Man at all Times gave us proof of his firmness and determined Resolution to do his country's service and to honor himself.

The Capts. named the river nearby Floyd's River and

the hill Sgt. Floyd's bluff. He is the first American soldier to die west of the Mississippi. We shall all miss him.

Aug 22, '04.

Tonight after our supper we held an election for a Sgt. to take the place of Sgt. Floyd. Each private had one vote. Drewyer gave as his opinion that Pat Gass was the Man for the Post, such is Drewyer's influence that Gass received 19 of the 24 votes and was declared elected. Capt. Lewis pronounced himself well pleased with the result. He notes that this is the first Election ever held west of the Mississippi River, he is certain that the great friend of democracy and the author of our Enterprise Mr. Thomas Jefferson is certain to be pleased also.

Aug. 26, '04.

At breakfast this day Capt. Lewis instructed me to go with Drewyer to hunt up our three Indian ponies that have strayed. We need them to bring in the meat. We took along our knapsacks, it frequently happens that the hunters get too far separated from the Party and must make their own camp on the prairie. Drewyer sent me East, he went south to search for the horses.

This is a fine open prairie. Deer, elk, buffalo, wolves are to be seen in every direction.

I searched the whole of the day, but found neither horse nor sign of one. I returned to the river but could not find Drewyer or the Party. I shot a duck for my supper and am pleased that I brought along mosquito brier which relieves me of these troublesome pests. I fired three shots three times but received no answer.

Aug. 27, '04.

This morning I worked up river, I found the first Indian pony and got a halter on him. I saw no sign of Drewyer or the Party, I begin to fear the Party has gotten ahead of me. I shot and roasted a deer. This was my last ball.

Aug. 28, '04.

I jerked some of the deer and bring it along. Today I found and caught a second horse, but not Drewyer or the Party. No sign of the Sioux Indians, this is their country and I am much afraid.

Aug. 29, '04.

I could not catch up to the Party. Tonight I ate the last of my deer. If I fail to catch up I shall be in an interesting situation. I am surrounded by meat but can kill none for the want of balls.

Aug. 30, '04.

Rode up the river all day no sign of the Party. One of the horses looks poorly, his eyes and nose runny. Suppered tonight on grapes only which gives me loose bowels.

Sept. 1, '04.

The horse died today, he was unfit for use he had worms. I am sore, fatigued, and weak from the want of meat. I must catch up with the Party soon or suffer the Consequences.

Sept. 3, '04.

Woke to discover two deer and three elk grazing with my horse not 20 feet from me. I had no means of killing them which frustrates me. I have my gun, powder, Mr. Boone's knife, and a horse to ride and meat for the taking, but without balls can get nothing. I tried rushing on the smaller deer with my knife but could not get close.

I grow weak on this diet of grapes, today I could scarcely ride the horse the diarrhea is so bad.

Sept. 5, '04.

More game, there is antelope among the buffalo, in addition deer and elk, but nothing for me to eat but plum and grapes. The Wind shifts to the North it is cold tonight.

I discovered some wild onions today which I eat, but I grew sick and puked them up.

Sept. 6, '04.

At dawn I saw the three biggest rabbits ever I saw. They were in a copse of cottonwood trees. I recollected that Drewyer related that once in an emergency like mine he had used a willow branch in place of his ball. He doubled up on the powder and the willow branch flew from the rue and with it he stunned squirrel.

I cut the straightest Willow I could find, crawled

close to the rabbit which was feeding and shot him fair in the head, he fell over stunned. I ran up and grabbed his foot just as he come to. I cooked him on a spit, this rabbit is large. Weight 7 lbs., the ears and feet large. I held back half of the meat for the morrow and proceeded up river but no sign of the Party.

Sept. 9, '04.

My dilemma grows. I reason with myself all day, if I fail to kill my horse for the meat I shall starve. If I kill the horse that is abandoning all hope of ever rejoining the Party, I will be alone and defenseless on this prairie with no means of fight when the Sioux find me.

Sept. 10, '04.

I have come to the conclusion that it is hopeless trying to catch up. I must wait here on a point in the river and interrupt a trading boat coming down from the Sioux or Mandan villages. I can get some ball and powder from them, then my problems will disappear. I can catch up with the Party when my strength returns.

Sept. 11, '04.

At noon today I heard shouts just around the bend below, this was no imagining or vision. I jumped on my horse and rode hard, to my inexpressible joy there was the Boat and pirogues pulled over, the Party was nooning it at the bank.

All rushed up to meet me demanding to know where I had been etc. I demanded to know where they had been, why did none come looking for me?

They did, Colter insisted. Every day a man went out to look, but he always went down river as they were certain I was behind.

Capt. Lewis said it gave him Delight to see me again, that it provides him much Relief, my being the Youngest and all. He allows me to eat a bit of buffalo hump only, too much he says shall make me sick. Colter brings me a bunch of grapes for desert, I throw them in his face which brought on general merriment, soon we commended a grape throwing contest. Damn me, but it is good to be returned to these fellows.

CONFRONTING THE SIOUX

Sept. 16, '04.

Drewyer took Colter and me hunting today, this is more sport than Labor, we killed nine deer and two buffalo of which we bring to camp the humps, tongues, and marrow bones only. From one of the bluffs we have a view that extended in all directions, so far as the eye can see in this pure dry air in that entire extent there were buffalo, deer, elk, antelopes, and wolves in immense numbers.

One of the deer Colter killed was the largest any of us has yet seen. Also remarkable it has a black tip on its tail, its ears are enormous. Capt. Lewis names it the mule deer for its ears. Drewyer says no man will ever again see such hunting, that not even Mr. Boone ever saw such a paradise.

There is a cactus in this country that is called a Prickly Pear, this is an accursed plant which sends sharp spikes into our feet when we step on it which is often as it nearly covers the ground. My moccasins which are a double layer of buffalo hide, not deer hide, are nevertheless not able to turn back these spikes. My feet are excessively sore.

Sept. 25, '04.

A Sioux Indian boy ran in at dawn, the Chiefs and warriors will be up shortly was his message. We raised a Flag staff and made an awning on a sandbar in the mouth of the Teton River. At noon two Chiefs came in with near 50 warriors. We gave them elk meat which they accepted, they give us great quantities of buffalo, some of it spoiled. Capt. Lewis gave a speech. We are here as Friends, he said. He explained Who we Were and Where we were going and Why.

Next he began to distribute presents to the Sioux. The first chief, Black Buffalo, he gave a medal, a red military coat, and a cocked hat. To the second chief, the

Partisan, he gave a flag and a mirror. Capt. C. marches us back to the pirogue. As we prepare to embark one Chief, Black Buffalo, grabbed the table of the pirogue and said that we should not go on, that we had not given enough presents. Capt. C. declared hotly that he would not pay a Toll, he said he wished to show these savages some medicine. We thereupon invited the two Chiefs to join us in the pirogue and see the Boat. They readily accepted, a few of their warriors came along.

On the Boat Capt. C. shot off the bow gun, to his disappointment they paid but slight heed. Instead they begged whiskey. Capt. C. passed around a bottle, the Partisan then began pretending to be drunk, sucking on the bottle and demanding more.

At Capt. C.'s order we persuaded the Indians back into the pirogue and with Capt. C. returned them to shore. So quick as we landed three of the Partisan's warriors grabbed the cable, the Partisan staggered up against Capt. C. and said we should not go on until the poor suffering Sioux have sufficient presents.

Capt. C. declared, We must and shall go. Colter and me and Silas Goodrich in the red pirogue prepared our rifles to fire, meanwhile Capt. C. drew his sword, York who was beside him and had his blood up was ready to kill. The warriors on the bank commenced to draw arrows from their quivers. Capt. C. called out to the Party to prepare for combat and he told our interpreter Labiche to Tell those People we are not squaws but warriors.

My heart pounded so I feared all would hear. The prospect of combat set my back hair on edge, I felt a rush of hot blood to my head. I was prepared to do my duty, but I was frightened.

The Chiefs, seeing our resolve, changed their attitude and now begged to be allowed to spend the night on the keel boat with us.

Sept. 26, '04.

The Chiefs slept on the decks with us. This morning we hoisted the sail, they were astonished very much by it. We proceeded five miles, with Indians all along the banks watching. The Chiefs invited us to visit their village, to which the Capts. readily agreed. The natives greeted us with every show of affection. These people are small, dirty, and fond of dress. The men attach polecat skins to their moccasins, they wear leather leggings and shirts which are loose cut and fold over the shoulder, to these they attach porcupine quills, beads, & etc. They paint their faces and complete the finery with eagle feathers in their hair.

The village was swarming with the squaws, warriors, children, horses, and dogs. These dogs bark, the warriors kick them. The lodges of these people reach 30 feet into the air, they are built on a frame of pine covered with buffalo skins sewed together and decorated with paintings of hunting scenes, war parties & etc.

Coveys of children dash away as we approach. These children, many of them naked, giggle and point. One boy not yet ten years old shot a pup through the head with his arrow from 50 paces and brought him to us as a present. We would not touch it, we had Labiche inform that we do not eat dog.

Horses graze all around. Each warrior has his war pony tied to his lodge so as to be instantly ready for combat. This Village gives a most romantic appearance.

The squaws are exceedingly solicitous. Black Buffalo offered his squaw to Capt. Lewis, she made obscene gestures. He declined the favor. Labiche was much agitated, he said the Chief will take this refusal as a great insult. Capt. Lewis still refused, he led us out of the lodge.

Sept. 27, '04.

The Indians drew themselves up on the bank. Their purpose was, Labiche informs, to keep us from going on until we had distributed sufficient presents. Capt. L. then ordered all hands at their posts, we are to Stay alert. He instructs us to sell our lives dearly if the Sioux attack.

Sept. 28, '04.

The Indians never attacked. At noon Capt. L. gave us orders to prepare to depart. At this, Black Buffalo's soldiers took a hold of the cable and refused to let us go. Black Buffalo demanded that Capt. C. stay and give more presents. Capt. C. turned red. Colter said, Look out now, anything can happen, he is so mad. Capt. L. ordered us to hoist the sail which we did, but the Partisan's warriors grabbed the rope and held us, the Partisan demanded tobacco.

Give him some and let us get out of here, said Drewyer.

No, said Capt. L., we will not pay a tribute.

The Chiefs clamored for tobacco, their warriors were howling and making gestures. Capt. L. drew his Sword, he was ready to cut the cable. Capt. C. who was in the bow held the firing taper for the swivel gun.

I thought I was in for it now, I was to be a participant in my first fight. I was tense and scared and excited all at once. I gripped my rifle and chose the Indian I would shoot if ordered, but the Partisan looked at the swivel gun and Capt. C. holding the taper above it, and at near-thirty primed rifles pointed at him, and decided to back off. He ordered his warriors to their tents.

Sept. 29, '04.

An early start with breeze behind us, we proceeded on at a good rate. Indians appear on the banks asking to come aboard or begging some tobacco. We answer them curtly and keep to our task. Clark says he has onboard more medicines than would kill twenty such nations in one day. We tie up tonight at the head of an island and stay on the Boat.

WITH THE RICARAS

Oct. 5, '04.

Some little frost this morning. In the fore part of the
day three Sioux on shore begged some tobacco from us,
we ignored them. They hurl insults. Made 20 miles
today. Capt. C. rewards us with a glass of whiskey.
Cruzzate brought out his fiddle. York shows us how to
dance the Virginia Reel. Where did you learn that,
Colter asked, York replied that when he was a child he
and Capt. C. would watch the gentlemen and their
ladies dance and imitate them. Colter says he never
heard of a black man like that.

This evening is calm and pleasant. The smokers enjoy

their pipes, Labiche tells stories about the Sioux. This is the kind of an evening that leads me to say thanks to my God that I had the good fortune to serve on this Expedition.

Oct. 6, '04.

A difficult day due to the river being divided into numerous numbers of channels, so much so that Cruzzate can choose only with difficulty. He curses all day. Immense numbers of geese, swans, brants, pelicans, and ducks fly over us.

Oct. 7, '04.

An early start, we passed many abandoned Ricara villages today. Labiche informs that this was once a powerful People, that it had 19 villages of 50 lodges or more each. The Small Pox came, today there are but 3 villages. The Ricaras in early days were in control of a great stretch of this river. They gave corns and crops and could defend themselves from the Sioux, but today they are reduced to a state of Dependency on the Sioux who grow no crops. These people, the Ricaras are thus today the gardeners of the Sioux.

Oct. 9, '04.

A cold windy day. We enjoyed a day of rest by watching the Ricaras come to us in some of the most astonishing boats the Party ever saw. These boats resemble a walnut broke in half, they consist of buffalo skins stretched over bent willow sticks, they are called Bull Boats. These boats bob in the water like a cork but the squaws manage them without the least difficulty. Today I saw three squaws in one boat, we thought it would surely tip as the wind came up and there were big waves on the river these squaws paddled on without apparently noticing. The Frenchmen with us who were watching and who live all of their lives on the water were compelled to admit that they were impressed by this feat, that they themselves had tried and could not master the bull boats.

These squaws express much astonishment at the color of York's skin. These women are cleaner than those of the Sioux and better formed, some of the young Squaws are very handsome and clean. They wear moccasins with fringed leggings and shirts made of antelope hide with sleeves and tied at the waste with a rope. All this is decorated with quills and beads and is striking.

Oct. 10, '04.

We had a council today on the riverbank so the Capts. could give their speech about the Ricaras now having a new father and should make peace etc. After, we walked to the village to pay our respects. The Indian Children all run from York who pretends a desire to Eat them. The boys torment him from the rear, he chases them around roaring like a bear. Capt. C. ordered him to stop, he had carried on the joke too much and made himself more terrible than Capt. C. wished him to do.

Capt. C. observed York enter a lodge with a squaw by the hand. Well I never, he said, this time that York has gone too far. Capt. C. went to the lodge where the squaw's husband stood guard. Capt. C. tried to tell the warrior he wished to enter the lodge to retrieve York. The man refused to budge. York was here by his invitation and that he was standing guard to prevent any interruption until York was through. He explained that York was big medicine, that the Ricaras want that medicine for themselves, that the only way they get it is by having their wives lie with York that they then absorb York's medicine from the wives.

Well I will be Damned, said Capt. C., as he walked away.

WINTER WITH THE MANDANS

Oct. 27, '04.

At 3 o'clock we came to opposite a Mandan village and sent out runners to bring in the chiefs. There are five villages in this area, they are scattered along the Missouri on or near the mouths of the Knife and the Heart Rivers. Three of these villages are Mandan, two are Minnitaree, with some 400 lodges and 4,000 people.

Today Capt. L. took me to accompany him on a walk to one of the Minnitaree villages where there was a man named Charbono, a Frenchie, who can speak Mandan and Minnitaree and a little English, so we are told. He lives with these People. Capt. L. desired to hire him as interpreter.

Capt. L. said while we were walking that he wanted me to know that he has kept an eye on me that I was becoming a soldier and was a good boatman and a promising hunter, and that he had noticed that I had been Sensible and stayed away from the squaws. He was, he said, well pleased with how I was doing that he had doubt due to my age but he was glad to say those doubts were now banished. My heart near burst from pride.

Nov. 4, '04.

Cutting and sawing all day to make our fort. At 2 o'clock Charbono came into our camp, he had been told Capt. L. desired to talk with him. With him he had his squaw, a girl of about 14 years of age who is pregnant. She is a Shoshone Indian from the Rocky Mountains. Charbono bought her from the Minnitarees, who captured her four summers passed along with her younger sister and some others. He answered Capt. C.'s question saying that he could not speak the Shoshone language but she, his squaw, could speak Shoshone and Minnitaree. He could speak Minnitaree and French. The Shoshones, he said, had many horses. They could help us make our portage over the mountains from the Missouri to the Columbia.

Nov. 3, '04.

Today we raised the walls of our huts. Sgt. Gass curses the cottonwood and prays God for some good Kentucky oak. The walls are up and firm and on the morrow we raise the Roof. The weather chill, there is not a man of us who is not dreading the winter. Charbono reports it gets so cold your pee freezes before it reaches the ground.

Nov. 11, '04.

Today Charbono brought his squaw and her sister to live with him in his Lodge, which he situated just outside our fort. At dusk Drewyer and I paid a visit.

Charbono is a skinny little man with a pocked face, he dresses like an Indian. His mother was a Chippawa, his father an Engagee. He is 34 years of age, he thinks. He was born in Montreal. Ten years ago he came to live with the Minnitarees. He purchased both the Shoshone squaws, but he now feels too old for two wives, he cannot satisfy both, he said, so he intends to give up the young one before she reaches her age.

The squaws' names are Sacajawea, which means Bird Woman, and Peme Bon Won, which means Stays With Her. These squaws are handsome and clean, one more so than any other I have seen. She, the younger one, is shy and looks at the ground, but her eyes when she looks up are like a fawn's, big and brown.

Dec. 2, '04.

A sharp cold day, zero at dawn. Mandan Chief came to see us, he informed that a large drove of buffalo was near and his people were waiting for us to join them in the chase. Capt. L. took 15 of us and joined some 40 Indians, all mounted bareback. There was a herd of buffalo grazing on the high prairie ground. We took stations and the Mandans rode off, saying they would stampede the game toward us.

In half an hour the herd was moving toward us, the Indians closing in on it from three sides. Shortly the bulls were running, then galloping. We each shot at a beast as they thundered past but only managed to bring down ten. I fear I am among those who missed, the air is so cold that despite my buffalo robe mittens I can not hold my rifle straight.

These Indians are the most wonderful horsemen.

When they get near the buffalo, riding at full speed, they drop their halter and guide their ponies with their knees only, using their hands to notch the arrows and shoot. This is done bareback. The ponies are trained to ride right beside the buffalo, a little back from his right ear, matching him stride for stride. The hunter then shoots downward into this bull's lungs. I never saw one rider fall off, nor did a man miss his quarry. Twice I saw men shoot their arrow clean through the buffalo.

Dec. 25, '04.

No Indians allowed in the Fort today. We tell them it is our big medicine day. Our Christmas feast is truly sumptuous, it was squash and beans, corn, the hump and tongue of fresh-killed buffalo, the steaks of antelope and strips of the back meat of the deer, all with great heaps of gravy and prairie vegetables which Sacajawea and Peme provide. We had dried apples and cherries to give us tarts for desert, which was fine.

Jan'y 1, '05.

We ushered in this day with the discharge of the cannon twice. Mandan Chief invited us all over to his village to play the fiddle and dance for his people, which we did to their vast amusement. Colter danced on his hands to general delight. Capt. C. permitted York to Dance which amused the crowd very much and somewhat astonished them, that so large a man should be so active.

After the dancing the men disappeared into lodges. One squaw, short and ugly and dirty, grabbed me by my member. I pushed her away and blushed. The old hag started cackling and pointing to my member and indicating that it was small, which made me blush more. Sacajawea spoke sharply to the woman who slunk off.

Sacajawea then led me off to the edge of the village where one lodge stood all alone. She tried to tell me something about this lodge and Peme, but I could not make it out. Later Drewyer explained that the Lodge is the one set aside for women when they have their menses. He said Sacajawea meant that Peme would soon be going there. That means she's going to be a woman soon, boy. And I have seen the looks she gives you. Think you are ready for her?

I think about it all the time.

GETTING TO KNOW PEME

Jan'y 2, '05.

Today I killed a beautiful white hare which was large.
Peme showed me how to make mittens out of it.

Jan'y 10, '05.

This day is my 19th birthday. I had mentioned this to
Colter, which was an effort, for he told everyone and at
dawn I was awakened by the Party with birthday
greetings and a volley and much joking about being the
Baby of the Party.

Capt. L. gave me permission to visit the Minnitaree
village, as I gathered my knapsack Colter called out,

Look out Peme, Here he comes. I come near hitting him, but I was too happy to fight.

The Indians were holding their buffalo dance when I arrived. I was startled to see Charbono standing before me with Peme. She smiled at me. My knees knocked each other. Charbono assured me that this was his and Peme's dearest wish. He indicated that she and I should go to a lodge. The drums beat strong. Peme smiled and used one of the English words she has learned, Come. She gave me her hand and led me off. I stumbled after her, my head was spinning. We entered the lodge.

We lay together on buffalo robes. She opened her robe, her breasts were small, the nipples soft and dark like a doe's nose. Her hair grows over her private parts, the sight of it caused my member to swell and jerk. She loosened her hair, sighing and smiling. I took off my leggings, my member stood up for her to see. She laughed and pulled off my shirt. She grabbed my member and began to stroke, to my embarrassment it shot off. She laughed again and stroked my face, soon my member was swelling and jerking again. She grabbed my member and pulled me to her, all Heaven broke loose. As she wiggled herself between my legs her face lit up, her breath was hot on my face. I near fainted it was so fine.

We fell asleep together, I was so happy. Happy Birthday to me, I thought.

Jan'y 15, '05.

A War Chief today told Capt. L. he intended to set out on a war party to make war on the Shoshones and invited us to join him. Capt. L. is counting on getting horses from the Shoshones to get us over the Rocky Mountains. He advised against war. A young warrior who accompanied him stepped forward, he addressed Capt. L. If we are in a state of peace with all our neighbors, what would his nation do for Chiefs. Our Chiefs, he said, are now old and must shortly die and our nation cannot exist without Chiefs.

Capt. L. made no reply. Later he remarked he could think of no answer. It is a dilemma, these People choose their Chiefs by who is the bravest and collects the most scalps, without war parties they cannot know who should be Chiefs.

Feb. 11, '05.

The fore part of this day Sacajawea had her time come. I assisted Charbono, we build up the fire to heat the hut, so we were sweating but feeling helpless and awkward, we were in the way. Peme shoved us out and the midwife took over. She delivered a fine boy, Charbono is some set up, he crowed and danced & etc. Sacajawea is tired but well. The baby is sleeping. He is so tiny, hardly bigger than a pup, he has black hair. I never saw so young a baby before, his eyes are large. Charbono names him Jean Baptist—Capt. C. calls him Pomp.

March 3, '05.

Spring is approaching. The days warm a bit, the sky is filled with geese, duck, swans flying north. The river begins to break up on place. Capt. C. has set us to making canoes, which we hollow out of cottonwoods. Sgt. Gass instructs us in the use of the adz. We work with great care, these canoes must carry us to the Rocky Mountains.

March 6, '05.

This afternoon I slipped when hollowing out the canoe and cut my foot badly with the adz. York carried me to Charbono's Lodge, Peme wrapped the wound for me, I am relieved of all Duty for recovery. I discover that my eagerness to be off headed West again is very great, but I fear I shall miss Peme something fierce. I had never thought I would be so full of sentiment for an Indian. When I arrived here I thought Charbono and all the Frenchies were fools and bad men to live with Indians and have a squaw for a wife, now I'm not so certain. Peme certainly is easy and fun to be with.

March 7, '05.

I spend the day in Charbono's lodge. Peme and I play with Pomp. She is making moccasins for me, I made a rattle for Pomp.

April 2, '05.

I am to be a Father! Sacajawea informed me today, I scarcely know what to think of this monumental news. I ran to Peme to ask her if it is true, her eyes was sparkling, she nodded that it was so.

April 5, '05.

All the canoes are down at the river ready to go soon as they are packed. Today large numbers of squaws came over in their bull boats to say goodbye. Capt. C. gave us the after part of the day free, the men disappeared in various directions with the squaws.

Charbono and Sacajawea packed their belongings. They will sleep in the Capts.' tent with their son, they fashioned this tent out of buffalo hides in the teepee style. Tonight I feel Peme's belly. I can feel nothing yet. She assures me that the baby is there and growing. I am eager to get going to continue our Adventure, at the same time I wish to remain here to see my Baby.

April 7, '05.

All the fore part of the day we adjust baggage. At 4 o'clock all was ready. The Crew shoved off in the keelboat, turning her bow downstream for the first time in her life, she is heading for St. Louis, carrying the Capts.' reports, artifacts, maps etc. from St. Louis to Mandan. When the boat turned down river and disappeared around the bend Capt. C. gave a signal and we pushed our canoes out into the river. Our fleet consists of six canoes and the red and white pirogues. Our Party consists of two Capts., three Sgts., and 28 men. In addition there is Drewyer, Charbono, Sacajawea, Pomp, and York.

As we passed the first bend, Peme was standing on the point waving to me. My heart sank. Captain Lewis's dog Seaman barked loudly. I signed to her that I would be back soon. She cried, something I had never seen her do. The sight of it made me cry. I will miss her not just for the sport either, I shall miss her, not just for the Baby either.

Tonight Capt. L. was writing in his journal. Silas Goodrich asked him if he would tell us what he wrote about this momentous occasion. He said he would, we gathered around, he read the following: This little fleet although not quite so respectable as those of Columbus or Capt. Cook, were still viewed by us with as much pleasure as those deservedly famed adventurers ever beheld theirs; and I dare say with quite as much anxiety for their safety and preservation. We are now about to penetrate a country at least two thousand miles in width, on which the foot of civilized man has never trodden; the good or evil it has in store for us is experiment yet to determine, and these little vessels contain every article by which we are to expect to subsist or defend ourselves. However, entertaining as I do, the most confident hope of succeeding in a voyage which has formed a darling project of mine for the last ten years, I can but esteem this moment of my departure as among the most happy of my life.

Colter asked, What about us, are we not in your Journal?

Capt. L. smiled and read on: The Party is in excellent health and spirits, zealously attached to the enterprise, and anxious to proceed; not a whisper or murmur of discontent to be heard among them, but all act in unison, and with the most perfect harmony.

We all applauded, a strange sound in the Wilderness, and went to our beds full of confidence in ourselves and our Capts.

A HUNTER'S PARADISE

April 8, '05.

A cold day. We made 15 miles.

April 9, '05.

The current strong, but we proceed on well, made 23 miles today. The stiffness gone from our Shoulders and we get into a rhythm that makes paddling the canoe seem more enjoyment than work.

When we made camp, Sacajawea busied herself in searching for the wild artichokes which the Mice collect. They deposit these roots in large hoards under the driftwood. She penetrated the earth with a sharp stick, by this method she soon procured a good quantity of these roots, which we all ate with pleasure, the flavor resembles that of the Jerusalem Artichoke.

This country is entirely destitute of timber. We use the buffalo chips for our fire.

April 23, '05.

Another 23 miles yesterday and 24 today. The country the same as usual, broke, treeless, desolate. This evening at our campsite we saw many tracks of the grizzly bear, these tracks were an enormous size, bigger than buffalo's tracks. Drewyer announced himself anxious to meet these gentlemen. Frasier was not. He said the Mandans had told him that these bears are ferocious beasts, that the Indians never go for them except in parties of ten warriors and even then they are frequently defeated with the loss of one or more of their Party.

Drewyer admonished us to recall that these Indians attack this beast with their bows and arrows, and their indifferent rifles with such uncertainty that they frequently misfire their aim and thus the Hunters fall sacrifice to the Bear. With Kentucky rifles, he said, we have nothing to fear. I rather think Drewyer is right that the animal has yet to be born that can stand to a Kentucky rifle.

April 17, '05.

Made 19 miles yesterday, 26 today. The country is as usual, except that the grass begins to green and the animals have appeared in great numbers. Immense herds of buffalo, elk and antelopes along the Shore. The buffalo is always accompanied by a parcel of their faithful Shepherds the wolves, who are ever in readiness to take care of the maimed, wounded, etc. Swans, geese and ducks in great numbers. Drewyer gets two each night.

April 21, '05.

The game continues in astonishing numbers. The buffalo begin to have their calves. The meat of these calves, which we had tonight is the equal of any Veal I ever tasted. This game is so plenty and tame that we go up near enough to club them out of the way; the club is indeed our weapon for getting the calves. Drewyer remarks that no man alive nor any yet to be born will ever see such hunting as this.

Nor eat so well, Colter says.

April 25, '05.

We are approaching the Yellowstone River. Capt. L. wishes to have time at the confluence of these two great rivers to take measurements. He decided to walk on shore to the main party and ordered the Fields brothers, Colter and me to accompany him. We were glad to get out of the canoe and use our legs rather than shoulders to proceed.

Capt. L., after six miles, led us on an ascent of the hills from whence we had a most pleasing view. With the valley of the Missouri stretching out to the west and that of the Yellowstone to the southwest, there was some little timber along their banks. These valleys are wide and fertile. The surrounding country is one vast sweep of grass, the whole of it coved with herds of buffalo, elk and antelopes. I clubbed a calf and Colter killed two cows of which we took the tongue only.

We proceeded on down to the bank of the river,

where we made the first camp any white man ever made on the Yellowstone. We are all in high spirits, Capt. L. the most so. Capt. L. ordered a dram for all; this soon produced Cruzzate and his fiddle. We danced with much hilarity. Capt. L. observed us, he said, with pleasure and pride. I overheard him remark to Capt. C. that the men seemed as perfectly to forget their past toils as they appear regardless of those to come. Capt. C. acknowledges that the men were alright.

April 29, '05.

This morning early Capt. L. and Drewyer were walking on the bluffs, they encountered a grizzly bear. They fired on him, notwithstanding that they each put a ball through him, he pursued Capt. L. open-mouthed and roaring for 70 yards. Fortunately he had been so badly wounded that he could not pursue so close as to prevent Capt. L. charging his piece. Both he and Drewyer fired again and dropped the monster. It was a yearling male that weighed 300 lbs.

Drewyer said later it was no wonder the Indians fear these bears so, armed as they were with those indifferent rifles or bows and arrows. He thought in the hands of a skillful rifleman these Bears are by no means so formidable or dangerous as the Indians represent them to be. He confessed that it was astonishing however, to see the wounds they will suffer before they have been put out.

May 1, '05.

This after I went hunting. I saw no Bear, but I did shoot a bird of the plover kind previously unknown to any of us. Capt. L. took his measurements carefully, and an exact description, and preserved the skin for Mr. Jefferson and the American Philosophical Society in Philadelphia. He said it would make a most valuable specimen and that I should feel proud. Capt. C. stiles it the Missouri Plover.

May 5, '05.

This evening after dinner we saw a grizzly bear on a sand beach down from us. Capt. C. and Drewyer went to kill the bear. They got on a ledge behind and each fired five balls into the bear, they are our best Marksmen and all ten balls found their mark, five went through his lungs. Notwithstanding, the beast let out a tremendous roaring which was continuous. He swam to an island or rather a sandbar in the middle of the river where he continued his ferocious roaring for near half an hour before he succumbed.

Colter, Goodrich and I set out to bring him in. He all but filled our canoe. Colter had to swim back to camp. The bear stank in a most horrid way. This is a terrible looking animal. Capt. L. thought he would weigh 600 lbs., we measured the bear, it was eight feet seven inches from nose to hind feet, three ft. eleven inches around the neck, his talons, five on each foot, were near five inches. We cut him up and boiled the oil and put it in a cask for future use.

May 9, '05.

It is notable that the river here is as wide as it is at its mouth. This discouraged us. Rubin Fields today asked Capt. Lewis, Will this river ever have an end? It will, Capt. L. replies. Notice that she is much shallower, he says. We all begin to feel extremely anxious to get in view of the Rocky Mountains.

The buffalo is so numerous that the men walking on shore frequently throw sticks and stones at them to drive them out of the way.

May 11, '05.

Brattan shot a grizzly today, notwithstanding that he shot his through the lungs the bear chased him into the river. Drewyer and a Party tracked the Bear where they shot him twice in the brain. This finally killed the bear. This is the only shot indeed that will stop these monstrous Beasts, and it is rendered difficult by two large muscles on the sides of the frontal bone and the thickness of that bone.

Capt. L. confesses that he would rather fight two Indians than one bear, that these bears being so hard to die rather intimidates him. He orders that no man go out alone in these Plains where the Bears are so numerous. He says for himself he intends to act only on the defensive with these gentlemen.

Me too, I said.

Not me, Colter grunted.

So far as I am concerned, said Drewyer, it is War to the death.

The way I figure, said Frasier, these bears have already won.

May 12, '05.

Charbono, Sacajawea, and I took a walk along the bluffs this evening. Charbono remarks that he is considering returning to the Minnitarees, that the Capts. treat him like a Slave, that this river will never have an end, etc. Sacajawea and I attempt to pacify him. Instead he urges me to return with him, that I can live with Peme and enjoy the rich and lazy life of a white trader in a big village.

I am soar tempted. This going upstream is damnable fatiguing, I am tired all the time. I miss Peme more than I thought possible, she is only a squaw, I tell myself, yet I think of her often each day and every night. I worry about our Baby. Sacajawea tells me she will make a good wife and mother, this tempts me further.

But Sacajawea will not be a party to desertion, she tells her husband she wants to see her people the Shoshones and her old home and the great Ocean and that after that we can all go back in the Minnitaree camp together to live.

May 14, '05.

Our heroes got their chance at a Bear this afternoon, six of them led by Drewyer and Colter went out for a bear seen on the river. They got within 40 paces of him unperceived. Four fire on the bear, two reserved their fire. Two of the balls passed through his lungs, one in the shoulder and one in the head.

The monster ran at them with an open mouth. The two in reserve fired and struck the shoulders which retarded his motion for an instant only.

All six men were now in full flight. Two of them threw aside their guns and shot pouches and plunged into the River. The bear immediately plunged in after them, he was near catching them when Drewyer shot him through the brain and killed him.

This is Colter's idea of fun, it is not mine.

Charbono was at the tiller of the white pirogue today with the sail up. The wind switched, instead of heading the pirogue into the wind Charbono allowed her to fall off to broadside. The wind turned the pirogue, the sail was down in the water, Charbono was hanging on and crying to God for mercy. Cruzzate in the bow threatened to shoot Charbono if he did not take up that tiller and do his Duty, which he did.

Various articles floated free. Sacajawea in the stern with Pomp on her back calmly picked them up as they floated by, the Capts. are much satisfied, as they say, by her quick thinking and action.

May 20, '05.

At noon we came to at the mouth of the river coming from the larboard side, Capt. C. names this river Sacajawea River. This was in honor of her having saved his journals, maps, medicine and instruments when her husband overturned the pirogue.

May 26, '05.

Today walking among the Bluffs, Capt. C. saw the Rocky Mountains! When informed by his shout we all gave three cheers, there is much splashing and merriment, we are within view of the mountains.

Tonight Capt. L. had me accompany him to the Bluffs to see those mountains. They lay to the North/Northwest and they were covered at their tops with Snow. Well, George, he says to me, I feel a deep pleasure in finding myself so near the head of the heretofore conceived boundless Missouri River.

Then he grew depressed, his face sank, he remarks that he expected these mountains would present us with a snowy barrier that they looked to him to be much higher than the Blue Ridge Mountains which is clear of snow by this Season. He cheered, his face brightened, he said he always held it a crime to anticipate evils, he would believe it a good comfortable road until he was compelled to believe differently.

PENETRATING THE MOUNTAINS

May 29, '05.

We made 17 miles today, we past a river on the larboard side which Capt. C. names the Big Horn River. We passed on the starboard side a cliff under which there was a mass of dead buffalo, hundreds of them, their tongues taken only, they made the most horrid stink. The Indians drive them over the cliff. These Indians, Sacajawea informed after she examined their moccasin tracks, were Blackfeet. It is astonishing the things she knows.

We camp just up from the mouth of a creek, the Capts. name her Slaughter River, after the dead buffalo.

This is a handsome situation in a copse of a large cottonwood with a cliff opposite that produces an echo. Capt. Lewis's dog barks at himself.

This evening Capt. C. walked on the shore, he found wolves so stuffed with buffalo from the carcasses they could not move. He killed one wolf with his espoontoon, he says that was something he had never expected to accomplish.

May 30, '05.

Rained the fore part of the day, the wind violent until 11 o'clock, when we set out. The river has become much clearer, the current stronger, there are many rapids and shoaly places, we proceed only with great labor and difficulty. We must employ the cord although we can scarcely walk. These cords break several times, we tumble into the water, which is cold. We are prevented from wearing moccasins by the round stones which are slippery, meanwhile the sharp stones cut our feet. But the current is too strong for the paddles and the river too deep for the pole. Cold and more rain the wind dead on.

The hills and cliffs we passed today took on a most remarkable and romantic appearance. The limestone erodes into one thousand shapes and figures, here a building, there a wall, here a chair for a giant, there niches and alcoves filled with statuary, everywhere columns and pedestals both broken and erect.

These cliffs shine white in the sun, they give the appearance of ancient cities destroyed, such as Sodom and Gomorra or Babylon.

Around each bend of the river new scenes come into view, more and more they make me think of Hell.

We come in sight of a perpendicular wall 300 feet high not ten feet wide, as wide at the top as at the base. At the top in the extremity of this Wall there is a hole bigger than a man. Oh Captain, Colter exclaimed, let me and George Climb to it. We will catch up later.

Capt. C. said it was foolishness for men so fatigued as we but Capt. Lewis reminds him that we are boys in age, that we should have some entertainment.

We reached the Wall from the back side, all around it was gargoyles, nymphs and etc. We climbed up into the hole, it was scary, the drop was straight down. We had a view one mile down and near three miles up the river. The land beyond the cliffs is a broken treeless desert. Save for the river not one drop of water is to be seen in any direction save in the far distance where the snow sparkles on the Rocky Mountains. The river is a bright blue ribbon winding through a brown and grey landscape. The only green one can see is that of the little stands of cotton trees along the bank. The scene is pleasing to the eye, I wished I was an artist.

After two hours of examining the weird shapes of toadstools made of limestone, statues and streets and allies of a destroyed city and wondering if this really was once a city, it seemed impossible that nature could have created such a Place, we returned to our canoe. It was coming on dark, we paddled up stream, soon the moon was shining on the cliffs and river. In the moonlight what appears horrid and grotesque in the day becomes soft and enticing. We reached camp which was opposite another cliff which possessed a natural bridge which gives the appearance from a distance of the Eye of a needle. York joined us for a climb to that Eye for the view which was very romantic.

Capt. C. complains that we are becoming a party of tourists.

June 1, '05.

We passed a cliff today that rivals the human art of masonry, it was one thousand feet long and more than 200 feet high, it contained uncountable numbers of the swallows nests made in a globular fashion. Those swallows were there in myriad numbers, picking mosquitoes and nats out of the air.

June 2, '05.

The hills give way today, the country becomes more level, the river widens with many islands. We make 19 miles by the cord. We came to on the port side opposite the entrance of a considerable river. The Capts. announce we will rest on the morrow as they will make observations.

June 3, '05.

An interesting question presents itself, as Capt. Lewis says, which of these two rivers is the Missouri? The left hand fork is the larger but its waters are clear. The right hand fork is turbid like the river below, it comes from the west where we want to go, while the left fork runs to the south. Mountains stretch from the SE to the NW.

As we dare not make a mistake so late in the season if we are to get over these mountains this summer, the Capts. have decided to explore both rivers by land to find the Great Falls, which the Minnitarees assure us are not far from the mountains and which are on the Missouri River. Capt. C. has selected me, Rubin and Joe Fields, Sgt. Gass and York to accompany him up the left fork. We spend the day mending our clothes, moccasins, etc.

June 7, '05.

We tramped these past three days over a dry hard plain, attempting to keep up with Capt. C. The country back from this River is level, yet we must ascend and descend steep hills and gullies to examine the river. Game of every description in numbers beyond description in every direction. Buffalo need to be shoved from our path. York tried to ride a half grown calf, he got thrown.

June 8, '05.

Capt. Lewis and his party not returned we begin to grow anxious. We passed the day with races and contests of wrestling and shooting. We have nothing to bet, the whiskey is near gone, still our competition is fierce. Colter and I together tried to wrestle York, he bested us easy.

June 9, '05.

Capt. Lewis returned. He agreed with Capt. C. that the left hand fork was the true Missouri despite that we ascended it near 40 miles without discovering the Great Falls. The men to a man disagreed with the Capts., only Sacajawea agreed.

We fear the left fork will terminate well short of the mountains and leave us with all this baggage far from the waters of the Columbia. Cruzzate spoke for us, he is a man of integrity and has great knowledge and skill as a waterman. He is firm of the belief that the right hand fork is the right fork.

Capt. Lewis said he would proceed ahead over land with a small party and continue on until he reached the Great Falls or the end of this river so if he was in error to be able to detect it and rectify it so soon as possible.

Capt. Lewis names the right hand fork Maria's River for his cousin Miss Maria Wood.

June 12, '05.

We set out early and proceeded well 18 miles. Rattlesnakes very common, as I lay reclining on the bank at noon, my head near a bush, a rattler near bites me, I cut off his head with Mr. Boone's knife.

Sacajawea very ill, so much so that Capt. C. places her in the stern of the remaining pirogue, here she has an awning for shade. Charbono much agitated. Sacajawea loses her senses and cannot speak, her arms and legs twitch, she does not eat. Charbono holts Pomp to Sacajawea's breast to feed. He does not get enough, he cries, which gives us all a feeling of helplessness.

June 14, '05.

Sacajawea cries out all night, her situation is alarming in the Extreme. Charbono wants to take her back to the Minnitarees, he says these Capts. know nothing about medicine, that what she needs is a

Medicine Man. I tell him to trust the Capts.

Progress slow today, we make but 10 miles only.

At four o'clock Joe Fields comes back from Capt. Lewis with a letter for Capt. C. Well Boys, Capt. C. calls out, this letter is dated from the Great Falls of the Missouri River. We are on the right fork.

We all cheered this welcome and unexpected news. Well I will be damned, says Cruzzate.

June 15, '05.

We put our backs into it today for fair, we were in sound of the Falls. Still we made but 12-3/4 miles only. Pulling these boats up the current so close to these Falls causes a fatigue which is incredible. We are in the water from morning until night, hauling the cord, walking on sharp rocks and round slippery stones, which alternately cut our feet and throw us down.

But we are in sound of the Great Falls never before seen by civilized man and our object for these past two months of unrelieved toil. It is thrilling to be here, my spirits soar to the sky. I am pleased and proud that I spurned the temptation to desert as there is no other place in the world I would rather be than here.

Sacajawea much worse this evening. Capt. C. and Charbono exchanged hot words, Charbono confessed to Capt. C. that Sacajawea had an infection in her parts.

Why in Blazes didn't you tell me that before, Capt. C. thundered.

She is my wife, replied Charbono.

Well you are a damned fool, said Capt. C. He made a poultice of the bark of the willow tree, he had her drink some of the juice and applied the bark externally to her region.

Charbono is furious but he knows Capt. C. is right. He is near beside himself with worry. So are all of us. Pomp cries from hunger which adds a great weight to our worry.

York killed a buffalo cow which had a calf, he drew the milk from her, Capt. C. feeds it to Pomp by dipping his little finger in the milk and giving it to Pomp to suck, this helps some.

June 16, '05.
Sacajawea out of her senses today, high fever, heavy sweating followed by chills. Capt. C. gives her medicine,

he is furious with Charbono for disguising her illness for so long. If she dies, he tells Charbono, it will be your fault.

Capt. Lewis joined us on this afternoon, he informed that there are not one Falls but five. The portage will be difficult and long. Capt. Lewis sent Colter and Drewyer to examine, they reported that two deep ravines cut the prairie in such a manner between the river and the mountains as to render a portage in their opinion for the canoes impossible.

Then we must do the impossible, Capt. C. declares. He put Sgt. Gass, Shields, and four other carpenters to work on making wheels from the cotton trees so as to provide carts for the portage.

June 17, '05.

I spend the day hauling canoes up a stream on the larboard side to the spot we will begin our portage. This is a rapid mountain stream full of rocks, we near overset twice.

Capt. Lewis has replaced Capt. C. as the doctor for Sacajawea. He continues the doses of bark but adds two doses of opium and laudanum to the poultice. I informed him there was a sulphur spring just across the river, he sent me over to bring him two gallons, he caused her to drink this mineral water which smells horrid. At noon he adds 15 drops of the oil of vitriol.

This morning her pulse was irregular, her arms and fingers twitching, Charbono cried out, Oh God, Please do not take Her from me. But the sulphur water appears to have answered her problem, this evening her pulse is regular, her breathing calm, her fever gone, she produces a gentle sweat. She is hungry, Capt. Lewis permits only a bit of boiled buffalo and a rich soup of the same meat.

July 2, '05.

This morning the Capts. took a party of 12 men for a frolic, as they called it, to an island they named White Bear Island from the great number of bears on it. They asked did I wish to come, No I said. Colter went. The Party killed three grizzly bears, only two men got chased into the water, one was Colter. Drewyer rescued him. This is the Capts. idea of a reward for all the hard labor of the past two weeks. It is my idea of damned foolishness.

July 4, '05.

Our dinner befit the day, the Capts. opened the stores, we had bacon, beans and coffee, all rare treats, in addition to our usual fare which is elk, deer, beaver, and buffalo.

Tonight the Capts. passed out the last of our Stock of Spirits in honor of our nation's 29th birthday. We were all soon drunk on one gill only. Such is the effect of prolonged abstinence. Cruzzate played the fiddle, York led us in Virginy Reel, we were merry.

July 12, '05.

All at work, making canoes, moccasins, shirts, leggings, and etc. or drying meat. Capt. Lewis says as we enter these mountains the game will grow scarce, we must prepare now whilst we are in the paradise for the hunter. We eat an immensity of meat, it requires four deer, or an Elk and a deer, or one buffalo to feed us for one meal only.

July 19, '05.

We set out early, the current strong, some rapids.

This evening we entered the most remarkable cliffs that we have seen yet. These rise perpendicularly from the water's edge to 1,200 feet, they create a canyon that is near six miles long, dark and gloomy. In all this canyon there is scarce one single place a man might stand. The current not so strong that we could not overcome her with the paddle, which was necessary as the water was too deep for the pole and there was no chance at all of using the cord.

We proceeded until long after the moon come up. It shined on the water thus giving some light in this forbidding place. Near midnight we located a gulch on the larboard side where we make camp. Capt. Lewis names this place from its singular appearance The Gates of the Rocky Mountains.

July 25, '05.
We proceed on tolerably well. Capt. C. has gone ahead on the land to search for the Shoshone Indians. Capt. Lewis assures us we are near the end of this river, he encourages us on occasion by taking up a pole himself, we tell him he is good with the pole, but in truth he handles it like an officer.

MEETING THE SHOSHONES

July 27, '05.

We set out at an early hour, proceeded on but slowly, the current rapid, it requires the utmost exertion. Even men so strong as we have our limits, Colter complains to Sgt. Ordway. Shut up you little bugger, Sgt. Ordway replies, and pull damn your ass pull.

The Cliffs hemmed us in for four miles until 9 o'clock when at the junction of three great rivers which has cut their way through a limestone cliff of 100 feet the country opened suddenly to extensive and beautiful prairie and meadows which are surrounded in every direction by distant and lofty snow covered mountains. Suddenly there was green to be seen in all directions, this is the most green we have seen by far since the early spring of this year. This is truly an oasis, it is most pleasing to the Eye.

This is the Three Forks of the Missouri River so long sought, we gave a cheer, it rang out loud and true.

Our campsite, which was directly below us, is precisely on the spot that Sacajawea was taken prisoner. I asked her to tell me what happened.

Below you is a place holy to the Shoshone, Flathead, Crow and other Nations, she replied. Since ancient times our people have come here to hold our dances and tell the old stories. Here we have rivers to swim in and meat to eat and here we can spread our offerings to the Spirits. Here we Play with our relatives and allies. We go to the caves in these cliffs where we paint our stories on the walls and the old ones tell us of former times, where the Shoshone came from and the battles that have been Won, and the lives of our Great Chiefs.

At this holy place, she said, it was a sunny warm summer day, this was seven summers past, she was eight years of age, Peme was seven years, they and all the children were playing in the river, splashing and swimming. None expected any trouble, all was peace.

Suddenly, those thieves the Minnitarees come riding over that cliff opposite, down on our camp on the river, they were screaming and whooping and shooting off their guns, our warriors had no guns, they fought with their arrows, the mothers ran to us to gather up their children to flee, my mother was carrying Peme whilst I ran beside her, a bullet hit her in the back of the head and it blew her head away. Peme fell, she was crying. The Minnitarees were all around us, some of our People who could get to their horses were fleeing up the river.

Those Devils killed the storytellers, stole the horses, burned our village, and made slaves of six of us children. They marched us to their village, it took near a moon, they scarcely gave us food or water, three of the children died, they beat us to break our spirits, we worked till we dropped, gathering Firewood and buffalo chips, cleaning hides, making moccasins, and etc. We slept in the open despite rain and hail and cold, we had no robes. Never have I been so hungry, tired, cold, or miserable.

When we reached the Minnitaree village it was some better, we did not have to march all the day, still I led the life of a slave, all the Minnitarees were free to beat us and make us work, they gave more food to the dogs than they did to the children of the Shoshones, frequently Peme and I fought the dogs for the bones. I feared for Peme's life and my own.

Sacajawea turned to Charbono. He rescued me, she said, he purchased me and Peme from the Minnitarees and became our protector and provider, we moved into his lodge where we ate good and slept with a robe and had skins for clothes and cannot be beat.

Old Charbono really does have an affection for this woman, he was crying to himself. He said it was truly distressing to see Sacajawea and Peme when he beat them, the memory of it made him sad.

Sacajawea recovered herself. All is well now, she said, she was on her way to see her People the Shoshones, we would meet them soon. She was near finished her belt which is truly beautiful, it is patterns of yellow, red, and white beads on a base of blue beads. She further works on an antelope skin dress which is richly embroidered with beads, new moccasins too. She intends to show her People how she has prospered with the Minnitarees and the white men.

July 28, '05.

Capt. Lewis names these three rivers. None has a precedence, he says, so none can be the Missouri, he calls the left hand fork the Gallitin for the Secretary of the Treasury, the middle fork the Madison for the Secretary of State, and the right hand fork the Jefferson for the Father of our Enterprise.

This after Capt. Lewis had me accompany him for a stroll, we climbed to the cliffs to observe the course of Jefferson's river, it appears crooked and difficult. The scene was beautiful in the extreme. Capt. Lewis said he was pleased that I was here, that I had not turned back with the journals at the Falls, that I was essential to the progress of the Party so much so as any of the men, save only Drewyer.

I looked at the ground, I fear I blushed, my spirits soared above the mountains. I hoped he would never stop, he did go on, he said it was but two years ago this month that I come to him in Pittsburgh, that in that time I had become a soldier and a hunter and a frontiersman and a Man.

My heart near burst.

Aug. 2, '05.

A repeat of yesterday only worse. Made 15 miles. My body so sore I can scarcely write. Sacajawea assures we approach her people and the waters of the Columbia, she encourages us, we require it.

Aug. 9, '05.

I found the Party enjoying breakfast, I brought in the haunches of two of the deer, there was much relief expressed at my arrival. Lost again, George? Drewyer inquired. Capt. C. said they should put a bell around my neck. Colter wondered did I have my balls.

Damn you all, I cried, this is the Second Time I have had to find you.

In my absence Capt. Lewis has come in and set out again in his search for the Shoshones, leaving Charbono behind, Charbono, it appears fails to keep up, he is too slow.

Aug. 10, '05.

This river is horrid, it twists and turns, we pull five miles to make a 1/2 mile, the men to a man wish to end this navigation and strike out by land. Capt. C. says not yet.

Today we passed a Cliff 150 feet high which Sacajawea informs the Shoshones call the Beaver Head from its supposed resemblance to the head of a swimming beaver. She declares we are but two days overland march from the waters of the Columbia as the Indians travel it.

By God Captain, Colter exclaims, in two days on this river we won't make five miles. This river is already impossible to navigate, Cruzzate adds, and will only get worse.

Now boys, Capt. C. replied, just recall that the Shoshones travel with horses and until Captain Lewis finds those Indians and makes trades we have none. Besides, he adds, the Shoshones travel light, they have none of the encumbrances we do.

Well, we can leave some of these encumbrances in a cache, I said, to my own surprise, why should we carry these huge iron kettles across the mountains? And don't forget either, I added, these Indians travel with women and children. If they can make it in two days so can we.

No we Cannot, Capt. C. declared, his face was red and his body tense. We must and will go forward with the canoes and all their berth. We are not tourists, we are not here just to look at the other side, we must cross these mountains and travel on all the way to the ocean. We shall need these kettles and all our equipment to accomplish this task. Our gear and trade goods must be brought to as near the divide as possible, then we will portage them over. When the portage begins, according to Capt. C. we will be damned thankful we brought the gear by water so far as we can.

Aug. 14, '05.

This evening at supper Sacajawea dropped a piece of deer liver into the fire while passing it to Charbono. He cursed at her in French and struck her with his hand in her face, hard enough to send her falling backward into Capt. C. who was holding Pomp.

This was a shocking occurance, we watched dumbstruck, Capt. C. helped Sacajawea to her feet, handed Pomp to her, and turned on Charbono, he was a volcano in full eruption, a real Vesuvius.

Never strike this woman again, he Thundered, if you value your life.

Charbono was considerably shaken and chastised. I feel sorry for him, he has had to labor with us, he is too old and feeble for such exertion. He lost his temper, it is true, but this is not like him, old fool though he may be he does not beat his woman.

We are all of us on the edge of unwholesome acts so taut are our nerves.

Aug. 16, '05.

Tonight there was a regular chorus of complaint directed at Capt. C. Not a man among us can see any point to going on this way. As Shields said, We can wait here for Capt. Lewis and the horses.

Capt. C. says our Duty is unmistakable, it is to proceed onto the utmost of our capability and limit.

Captain, says Colter, I am frank to say I have long since passed my limit, I have no capability left.

Nor I, said I.

All said they are passed their limit.

Capt. C. said we could sleep late in the morning and

dismissed us. He is inhuman, inflexible, unreasonable, stubborn, the more so than any man I yet met. He is worse than my Father.

Aug. 17, '05.

We set out at 7 o'clock, Capt. C. walked on shore with Charbono and Sacajawea. She had put on her belt and new dress, she looked pretty and lovely. They proceeded but a short distance when Sacajawea, who was 100 yards in front, began to dance and show every marks of the most extravagant joy, turning round and pointing to several Indians on horseback, sucking on her fingers to indicate that they were of her native tribe.

The Indians came singing aloud, we all rushed to meet them. Drewyer, who was with those Indians, informed that Capt. Lewis was coming along with more Indians and horses, we pounded each other on the backs, we all cheered until we were hoarse.

When they came there was general hugging and embracing between the soldiers and Indians, dancing and whooping, and etc.

Capt. Lewis informs that the divide is not far, we

cheer again. The portage is an easy one, he says, up a valley of but gradual descent. But we must have horses, he says, in short we are dependent on these People. In three days with them he could not impress upon them what was needed by the sign language which did not answer. But now that he had Sacajawea with him he was ready to trade.

The chief, Cameahwait or He Who Never Walks, called a council. He had his warriors build a shade of willows. Capt. Lewis was seated on a white robe and the chief tied in his hair six pearls. All took off their moccasins, soldiers and Indians alike, as a pledge that if they fail to speak the truth in this council they will go barefoot on these mountains.

The smoking ceremony began, it took near an hour, when it finally ended Capt. Lewis, glad of an opportunity to be able to converse intelligently, sent for Sacajawea. She came into the circle, sat down, and was beginning to interpret when in the presence of Chief Cameahwait, she recognized her brother.

She instantly jumped up and ran and embraced him, throwing over him her blanket and weeping profusely.

The chief was himself moved though not to such a degree. After some talk between them she resumed her seat and began to interpret Capt. Lewis's speech to Cameahwait but her situation overpowered her and she was frequently interrupted by her own tears. Cameahwait had told her all her family was dead except himself and a son of her eldest sister.

When Sacajawea composed, Capt. Lewis told Cameahwait who we were, that we had come to help our friends, the Shoshones. He said we were preparing the way for a trading establishment where the Shoshones could obtain guns to defend themselves from the Blackfeet and Minnitarees, that the sooner we got to the Pacific Ocean and returned to St. Louis so sooner could the Shoshones have their own trading post. That it was therefore in the interest of the Shoshones to help us over the divide and to provide guides to the navigable part of the Columbia. That if Cameahwait and his People failed to help us over or sell us horses, No white man would ever again come to their country. That was his first wish was that Cameahwait should immediately gather so many horses as required to transport us over the divide to his village, which is on a branch of the Columbia where we could trade for so many horses as they could spare at our leisure.

Cameahwait in reply thanked Capt. Lewis, he said he would render every service. He lamented that it should take so long before a trading post could be established. He had not enough horses with him to carry us over the divide, but he would return to his village tomorrow and bring on all his People and Horses.

The Capts. then distributed presents, a medal for Cameahwait with President Jefferson's likeness, a uniform coat, a shirt and leggings, tobacco, and a knife. Then we all proceeded to hand out presents of paint, awls, knives, beads, mirrors, fish hooks and etc. They examined us with astonishment, they were much excited by our white skin under our shirts, our rifles, the canoes, the sagacity of Capt. Lewis's dog Seaman, York, both his size and color and hair, all in turn shared their admiration.

Capt. C. will go on foot tomorrow ahead with 11 men, their saws, adz and other tools, to the waters of the Columbia to make canoes if the water be navigable. The Indians warn that it is not. Notwithstanding this unwelcome news all are merry tonight. We dance with the Indians to their drums and Cruzzate's fiddle. Sacajawea dances with her friends, her happiness glows so bright as the fire. All admire her belt and dress.

I am happy for her and even more so for myself. At last we are done with this terrible river, whatever lays ahead it cannot be so bad as what we have been through.

Aug. 19, '05.

We set out early, soldiers, warriors, squaws, old people, dogs, horses, children, all mixed together. As we approached the pass Colter and me amused ourselves by jumping back and forth over the little rivulet beside the road. This entitles us to a Brag for the remainder of our existences, says Colter, viz. that we have stepped across the Missouri River.

He led us to the pass, I was eager to see the other side, the site staggered me. There are immense ranges of high mountains still to the west of us, their tops covered with

Snow. The Columbia must have a terrible time in finding her way out of these tremendous mountains.

We were all downcast.

We descended the mountain about 3/4 miles where we came to a handsome bold Creek of cold clear water running West. Here we first tasted the water of the Columbia. We proceeded on over a very mountainous country. We camped beside a Spring.

Aug. 20, '05.

The Shoshones are the poorest and most miserable nation I ever beheld. They are all near starved. They are rich only in horses, of which there are two for each person, or 800 horses and 400 people. They have but two guns amongst them, and this type of gun is an indifferent fuse.

Notwithstanding their wretched state of poverty they are cheerful, even gay, fond of gaudy dress, frank, fair in dealing, generous with the little they have, honest and not beggarly. These are, in short, a fine People whose want of guns for sustenance and defense is a catastrophe.

Capt. C. persuaded Cameahwait to instruct us with

respect to the geography of the country. The Chief drew a river with a stick in the ground, this was the river we were on. He made it flow Northwest, ten miles where it joined another river together they continue to flow Northwest one day's march, then West two days' march.

Here he placed a number of heaps of sand on each side, which he indicated were vast mountains of rock. He indicated that these mountains were inaccessible to man and horse.

Cameahwait said he understood from the Nez Perce Indians who were his allies with whom he sometimes hunted buffalos and who live on this river beyond the Rocky Mountains, that this river ran a great distance toward the setting sun and finally lost itself in a great lake of water which was ill-tasted and where the white men come in large boats.

My legs are sore, not from pulling canoes but from sitting on a horse. This country is intimidating, high rugged mountains are in every direction, all covered with snow. The Capts. got us so far, I figure they will get us the rest of the way, but I do wish I knew how.

OVER THE BITTERROOT MOUNTAINS

Aug. 21, '05.

Set out early with Capt. C. and Party to explore this
river to determine if it be navigable.

We encountered a small party of the natives who were
gathering a quantity of camas roots which they pound
and mix with berries and make a kind of bread, some of
which they give to us. It is insipid to the taste, but appears
capable of sustaining Life for some time, or so at least
Capt. C. tells us. This was our only food this day.

Aug. 23, '05.

We continue our investigation of this river, it appears
impossible. Today we proceeded 12 miles sometimes

following a wolf path at other times climbing over the rocks and mountains. This river is almost one continued rapid, the passage with canoes is utterly impossible and there are no trees to make canoes from anyway, the water is confined between huge rocks and the current beats from one against another. Nor is there any possibility of portage.

Below this point where we camp, according to Old Toby, our Shoshone guide, the river gets worse, the mountains close and perpendicular cliffs on all sides, the water runs with great violence from one rock to the other, foaming and roaring through rocks in every direction. The rapids which we have seen, are, Old Toby said, Small and trifling, we tell Capt. C. this route is no route at all, he agrees. We shall start back tomorrow so as to inform Capt. Lewis. All are sick, we have only Choke Cherries to eat today, it gives us the diarrhea.

Our spirits low, our hunger great. This is the first retrograde movement we have been forced to make in the past two years, it is discouraging in the extreme.

Aug. 25, '05.
Yesterday and today we have been in full retreat, this is humiliating. To add to our misery, we are near

starved. Today we met that same small party of Indians on the river, they gave us a little boiled salmon and dried berries to eat, about half as much as we could eat.

Sept. 2, '05.

Today we left the road which we are pursuing and proceeded up the NW fork of Louis River, there is no road on this fork, we were forced to cut a Road through thickets, over rocky hillsides where our horses were in perpetual danger of slipping to their certain destruction and up and down Steep hills.

At noon the horse I was leading slipped down a steep hillside, I lost his halter, he tumbled and turned, he broke his leg and his neck, he finally came to a stop some 400 feet below on a rocky ledge.

Capt. C. instructed me to retrieve his pack which I did only with the greatest difficulty, risk and etc. I could carry only the pack, the meat I had to leave behind, which was only with regret, as we are in desperate want of meat, even horse meat. I did not catch up to the Party until night fell. Nothing but dried salmon to eat.

Sept. 4, '05.

A very cold morning everything wet and frosted, the ground covered with snow. We ascended a mountain and took the dividing ridge and fell on the head of a Creek which we descended, it was a steep descent, still I should rather go down than up these mountains.

Tonight we came to a fork where we met the Flathead Indians who were on their way to the rendezvous with Cameahwait and the Shoshones. There were over 33 lodges or 400 people, they had near 500 horses. How they passed these herds over these mountains is a mystery to me.

We camped with these Indians which was friendly. Like us, they had no food, only berries, which they shared. My stomach growls like a bear, for the want of food, the berries give me the diarrhea again.

Sept. 5, '05.

Colter and a number of others pass the night with the squaws, I did not, I am much too fatigued and weak from the want of meat to want to make sport.

Sept. 8, '05.

We proceeded down this valley today, at noon Drewyer and Colter caught us up, they had killed an Elk and Buck on which we dined.

This valley grows even more beautiful to the eye but most depressing to the spirits, as we proceed we cannot help but glancing to our left which is west, the way we must go to the ocean, the sight is staggering. Mountains without end, all covered near to their base with snow, not a hint of a pass through these tremendous ranges, sooner or later we must turn from our northerly course and leave this valley and head west. None of us can imagine how we will get across these obstacles.

Sept. 9, '05.

At 12 o'clock we halted on a small branch where we breakfasted on three geese which Colter shot. Just as we set out again Drewyer came up with two deer.

We made camp on a creek that comes in from the west which Capt. Lewis called Traveler's Rest Creek as he has determined to halt there for a day of rest for our horses and to take some celestial observations.

Old Toby informs that here we will leave Clark's River and make our turn to the west into the mountains, following Traveler's Rest Creek to the dividing ridge, thence across the mountains to the prairie where the Nez Perce live.

This is a handsome situation, the water clear, the land fertile, the grass good for the horses, the scenery striking.

Boys, Capt. C. concluded, we will be over these mountains, in a week into the land of prairies where we can kill meat and build canoes and be waterborne again. He said it would then be an easy float to the Pacific Ocean and fat times for the winter.

Sept. 12, '05.

The road today through this Country is very bad passing over hills and through Steep hollows. What makes it so much the worse is the fallen timber which covers the road and forces us to step over and around, which is cumbersome and laborious when leading an Indian pony packed with goods. To add to our difficulties these packs are frequently caught in a tree limb, or knocked loose, which delays us.

Our guide caused us to leave the valley and cross a mountain eight miles without water with a long descent back to the creek. I was in the rear, I did not make it up to camp until 10 o'clock. I was famished, but Drewyer had managed only one pheasant. I eat berries.

Sept. 14, '05.

We proceeded up the creek valley, at noon we come to some Springs, the water was near boiling hot. Colter and me wished to stop to soak in the pool the Indians have made by placing rocks around the Spring, but Capt. C. said we had no time for such foolery.

We proceeded along the side of a Mountain leaving the creek to our left, at six miles we come to a beautiful and extensive open glade which was all bright blue, at first glance it appeared to be a lake. These glades were filled with flowers which was enchanting. The runoff from these meadows was to the west, that is where we are now over the dividing ridge that separates Traveler's Rest Creek and Clark's River from the waters of the river the Nez Perce call the Kooskooskee, which river flows into the Columbia. This creek we name Glade Creek.

We proceeded two miles and encamped opposite a small island at the mouth of the branch. The river is at this point eighty yards wide, swift, stony, and clear, in short, a bold, handsome river.

The branch that comes in at our camp we named Killed Colt Creek from our killing a Colt to eat. This meat was necessary if we were to continue on. No one likes the idea of eating horse meat, but it is sustaining and nourishing if illy-tasted. No men could do such excursions without meat.

The Mountains which we passed today much the worse than yesterday, this is due to their steepness to which is added the thickly strewn steep ascents and descents of the mountains stepping over so great a number of deadfall fatiguing the horses and men exceedingly.

Every bone in my body aches, I am cold and I am hungry, I am tired enough to sleep for a week, I have no alternative but to stick to the Capts. and hope that they can somehow get us through these mountains before we all starve, horses and men.

Sept. 15, '05.

After four miles down the river the road left the river to the left and ascends a mountain. It winds up in every direction switching back and forth to get up the Steep ascents and is covered by immense quantities of deadfall. At noon we stopped to noon it at a Spring and let our horses graze.

This after we continued our route up the mountain, at 3 o'clock my horse slipped and rolled down a steep hill, I lost hold of his halter. He turned over and rolled down the mountain for 40 yards and lodged against a tree. His pack included Capt. C.'s writing desk, the Desk was broke, the horse escaped by a miracle without injury.

Colter, who was with me, we were in the rear of the Party, said, It would have been Better for you George if you had lost the horse and saved the desk.

We come to the camp only after dark, it was on the top of the ridge of the mountain, we discovered the Party had no water only melted snow and no meat, only two pheasants killed today. We cooked the remainder of the Colt and made our soup. Capt. C. excused the loss of the Desk, he said we were lucky we had not lost more.

We are all hungry, cold and miserable and exhausted. With the greatest exertion we made but 12 miles today. From our camp we observe high rugged mountains in every direction so far as we can see. Our situation is indeed forlorn.

Colter, I said to him tonight, I remember you saying that so long as we had powder and balls we could take on anything the Wilderness could offer. We have plenty of powder and balls, good rifles, and the best hunter in America, and look at us.

Well I was wrong, he grumbled, leave me alone.

Sept. 16, '05.

Snowed last night and all day. Snow six inches deep this morning and ten inches tonight. Our route continues up and down over steep mountains, we slip on the snow, the cold penetrates our shirts, my hands and feet are numb, I fear my feet will freeze in these moccasins. When we are on the trail we sweat in buckets, so soon as we stop we get chills.

Sept. 17, '05.

With the most incredible exertion today we made but 10 miles. Drewyer killed but a few pheasants which were insufficient for even a thin soup, thus the Capts. ordered another Colt killed. Capt. C. gives an extra portion to Sacajawea, who as he says eats for two. Her milk is thin. Pomp cries which is unlike him, it worries us.

Our spirits are low. We are all disheartened. This is worse than hauling canoes up Jefferson River, but with the difference that here no man is hard to complain, the reason being that there is nothing for us to do but continue on in the faith that Toby is right, that there will be an end to these Mountains some of these days.

Sept. 18, '05.

This morning early Capt. C. set out ahead with Drewyer and five additional hunters to carry on to the level country ahead and there to kill some game and send it back.

Sept. 19, '05.

Set out early, proceeded six miles through steep ascents and descents, the road bad, much deadfall, when we reach a high point which is clear of timber we see nothing but more mountains in each direction, this is disconcerting.

At noon the ridge we were following terminated and to our joy we discovered in the far distance to the West a large tract of Prairie country. Through this plain, Old Toby told us, runs the Columbia River. It appears 60 miles or more distant which is disheartening, but what is Satisfying is the knowledge that there is an end to this horrible mountain country.

We followed up a creek, this road was excessively dangerous, it was a narrow rocky path along the side of a steep precipice. Frasier's horse fell and rolled with his load 100 yards into the Creek down a perpendicular hill broken by large, irregular rocks. Frasier and I scrambled down the precipice to the horse full expecting him to be dead, we were astonished when we reached him to find him fine. We took off his load, he jumped up, shook himself and was ready to go. We loaded him and he did go on, it really was a wonderful escape.

Sept. 20, '05.

We eat a little bear's grease which was the very last kind of eatables of any kind we have. We set off at 10 o'clock having been detained by Colter searching for his horse which had wandered. At two miles we found a horse hung for us with a note from Capt. C. saying he had found this horse that had strayed from the Indians and that he had killed it for us, and that he was proceeding on in search of those Indians. We put the horse on back of our horse and proceeded over a mountain down a ridge to a Spring run. Here we halted and dined sumptuously on horse meat which provided much comfort to our hungry stomachs.

As we nooned it Capt. Lewis learned that one of the pack horses was missing, he sent Lapage who had charge of his horse to search for him. At 3 o'clock Lapage returned without the horse. Capt. Lewis was much put out as the horse was carrying his winter clothing and merchandise. He called me and Colter to him, he said we was his two best woodsmen (as Drewyer was the Capt. C.), he wished us to search for the horse while he and the Party proceeded on. Search until you find him, he ordered.

We got on two horses and set out, we searched along the trail until night but found nothing. We made camp on a small creek. We have nothing to eat.

Why can't Capt. Lewis use skins and furs like us for his clothes, Colter asked before going to sleep.

Sept. 21, '05.

We began our search at first light, it was arduous in the extreme, worse the second time on this trail than the first. At noon we were near collapse, there was not so far as we could see not even a bird. There was no other living thing than us.

At two o'clock we found the horse, which was a mean and angry horse that could not be caught until he got hung up with his pack in some timber. We got the pack off, the horse bolted, he ran so fast we had no opportunity to raise our pieces to fire on him.

Colter said we should go after the son of a bitch, that he would answer nicely for our supper. We will never catch him, I said, we must start back.

Damn, said Colter. He supposed I was right but he would count that damn horse the best meal of his life if he found him.

Sept. 22, '05.

At dusk we caught up with the Party, they were with the Nez Perce Indians on a prairie on the edge of these mountains. We were exhausted and fatigued and near starvation, but our spirits revived when Capt. Lewis gave us some bread made of camas root and some dried salmon which answered perfectly for our supper, we ate until we near burst.

A full stomach such as I have tonight is all that stands between a man and contentment. Colter and I contemplated our accomplishment, we have triumphed over the Rocky Mountains.

WITH THE NEZ PERCE INDIANS

Sept. 23, '05.

The Capts. held ceremonies today with the Nez Perce, informing them who we were and etc. The Chief, Twisted Hair, is an old man small of stature but large in his dignity. We traded with those Indians from our small stores of Merchandise, fish hooks, handkerchiefs and beads for quawmash roots which were dried and made into bread, or in their raw state, and Berries of red Haws, and dried salmon.

Capt. Lewis and Joe and Rubin Fields very sick this evening, this is a result, Capt. C. declares, of eating too much root too fast. He warns us to be moderate, to men as hungry as we this is rather like telling the river to stop its flow to the ocean. All ate heartily tonight.

These Indians spend most of their time procuring food. The Summer and Fall they are fishing for the salmon, in the winter they hunt deer on Snow Shoes in the plains and take care of their immense numbers of horses, and in Spring these cross the mountains to the Missouri to get Buffalo at which time they frequently meet with their enemies and lose their horses and many of their people.

Sept. 24, '05.

My bowels near burst, I could scarcely breathe last night from the gas, this morning I have a Lax and heaviness at the stomach, the dysentery is bad amongst all the Corps of Discovery, we can move but with great difficulty. Capt. C. administers Rushes Pills which causes explosions, it sounds like cannons going off all around our camp. Notwithstanding that the wind blows, the stink is constant.

We moved our camp to a small island on the Kooskooskee River, the Indians and their gangues of horses helped us else we could not have made it. Capt. Lewis scarcely able to ride on a gentle horse which was furnished by

Twisted Hair. Three times in two miles Colter and I were compelled to lie on the side of the road, we were groaning with pain in our stomachs and bowels. We are very weak, we stand only with difficulty and walk hardly at all.

Sept. 26, '05.

I am bloated like a catfish that has been left in the sun on the bank of the Missouri for five days. I stink, I swell, I shit, I lay down. It is the same with all of us.

Sept. 27, '05.

Capt. Lewis is very sick, he can scarcely move, his stomach bloated and much gas. Drewyer is sick. Capt. C. administers Salts, Rushes Pills, Jalap, Tarter emetic & etc. all of which makes us worse so far as I can see. Colter refused to take the medicine and he has gotten well, from now on so will I.

Sept. 28, '05.

My condition improves, I feel myself again. The bulk of the Party still sick. I worked on the canoes this day but made little progress.

Sacajawea and Charbono have also recovered, they were never so sick as well. Tonight I had the guard, I thought about the past days and wondered why these Indians had not taken advantage of our helpless situation and cut our throats and taken our rifles. We have more rifles with us than they shall ever see in their lives and enough powder and lead until Doomsday, they could have had it all. Indeed if they were to attack us tonight we could scarcely resist, only Colter, Capt. C., and myself are well.

When Colter relieved me on guard I talked with Sacajawea and Charbono, asking them why the Nez Perce failed to attack us. Sacajawea knew the answer, she said she had talked with an old woman who knew a little Shoshone. This woman had related that the Nez Perce had wished to kill the white soldiers, but as they were preparing themselves for a War, a squaw, whose name was Returned From a Far Country, came to them.

This squaw had been captured by the Blackfeet many years ago, then she was traded to a Frenchie and living among the Atsina. Her husband was a good and kindly man who treated her well, for some years they lived among whites. Two years passed her husband granted her wish and allowed her to return to live with her People. She had never forgotten the kindness of the white men.

So on this occasion, she addressed the warriors. These are the people who helped me, she said, indicating the white men. Do them no harm, she instructed.

The warriors thought this was great medicine at work. They took her counsel and took off their war paint and suffered us to live.

Once again, the Corps of Discovery had been saved by a woman, Sacajawea concluded. I could agree and be thankful.

Oct. 1, '05.

The most of the Party still sick. Those who are capable of work are too week and feeble to hack out canoes. Capt. Lewis has thus directed us to use the Indians' method, which is to hollow out the canoe by building a fire in the pit under the trunk.

The hunters, such as there are, have but small success. We have eaten crow, wolf, and Magpies and a pheasant, this is insufficient meat. This evening Colter returned with but one prairie wolf. The Party so weak Capt. Lewis concluded to kill a horse, which we did, it was in tolerable order, and we eat the meat with good relish, so much so as ever we did fat buffalo on the Missouri.

Oct. 4, '05.

The health of the Party improves, but we have nothing to eat today but roots which give us violent pains in our bowels.

Drewyer came in, he had killed nothing, he was heated up which is not like him, he never gets angry. Mon Dew, he said, I must have meat. He then traded some fish hooks and beads to an Indian for a dog, smashed the dog's head with his tomahawk, held him by a kind leg whilst he singed the hair off over the fire, popped him into the boiling kettle with our soup of quawmash roots, pulled him out after twenty minutes, split him in quarters, and shared him with Cruzzate, Labiche, and Lapage. They proceeded to stuff themselves with dog.

All of us who were not Frenchies puked at the site of this.

Oct. 5, '05.

Good progress hollowing out the canoes today. We round up our horses and branded them with stirrup irons, we have 38 in all, the sons of Twisted Hair promised to care for them until we return.

Capt. C. informs that by his calculations we came 160 miles from Traveler's Rest Creek. That is 160 miles of torture, it is disheartening to think that we must cross those mountains again to get home.

We purchase salmon and roots from the squaws for beads.

Oct. 7, '05.

We loaded all the canoes and at 3 o'clock set out for the Pacific Ocean. We proceeded on over a number of bad rapids, frequently our canoe runs fast on the rocks, we are obligated to get out in the cold water and haul her off.

Cruzzate gave Colter, who is in the bow, some

lessons on maneuvering a canoe in rapids, using his paddle to draw the nose this way or put her that way, whilst I use my paddle in the stern for a rudder or to pull or push. It is astonishing how maneuverable this Scout canoe can be, this is the first time we have gone down a Stream, it is necessary to make quick judgments, just one mistake will set us over. We can make her glance off the most of the rocks with just a twist or turn of the paddle.

Running with this strong current is great fun, the both of us shouting the whole time, missing but by inches huge rocks that would stove us in sure, the experience is exhilarating.

Oct. 8, '05.

Drewyer and Charbono traded for two dogs, the Frenchies have announced that they must have meat to live, that they cannot subsist on a diet of fish only. We watch them eat the dogs with relish, Colter and I agreed that on the morrow we will try dog meat.

How can you even think of eating dog? I can hear my mother asking. Have you forgotten Old Blue who was your constant companion of your youth? I reply that these are Indian dogs, not pets, that I must keep up my strength.

Oct. 9, '05.

We had a merry party tonight with Twisted Hair and his warriors and the Indians of this camp and ourselves. Cruzzate brought out his fiddle and we danced. The squaws were much impressed by York and his dancing, and as York likes to preen himself before the ladies we were all soon doubled over with laughter.

Suddenly a woman jumped into the circle and pushed York out and began to sing a sad song which Twisted Hair indicated, meant pity this poor Indian squaw. She then took up a basket of roots and began giving each white man some roots, signing all the while that this was all she had in the world. When she came to me I refused to take any from her, it was an embarrassment, poor as we are we are not so poor as her. Sacajawea told me to take the roots, but I would not.

The woman grew angry, she threw her roots into the fire, and took a sharp flint from her husband and cut her arms in Sundry places so that the blood gushed out. I was horrified already, I near fainted when she wiped up the blood and ate it.

She proceeded to rip off the beads and pieces of copper which hung about her and gave them out to the men around her, she saved the last bit, a sea shell, for me. I could not take it, I wanted only to crawl out of that Lodge. She went into a fit. She screamed and tore her hair by the roots.

Oct. 10, '05.

This country is desolate, there is not one stick of timber on it, with barren and broken prairies on each Side. The river is near 400 yards wide and of a greenish color. There are Indian's camps wherever there are rapids which is often one each mile.

Pomp can crawl now, he creeps around the fire and examines us, he is our great favorite. Tonight he reached into the fire, Capt. C. made to stop him, Don't stop him, Sacajawea indicated. Pomp burned himself and cried, Capt. C. asked Charbono why Sacajawea stopped him from stopping Pomp, Charbono explained that from now on the Baby will not reach into the fire, that this is the way the Indians let their children learn a lesson.

Oct. 11, '05.

Many rapids and fishing camps today. Cliffs and high prairie on each Side. This river is very handsome, the country pleasant but no timber, we can scarcely find wood enough to cook our victuals.

At 35 miles we came to a bad rapid which Twisted Hair warns us is very bad. We come to on the starboard side to view it before we attempted to descend through it, Capt. C. had made me and Colter go through it in the pilot canoe whilst he watched, we made it with some difficulty, we come near overturning twice. The Capt. determined to make camp where they were and run those rapids in the morning.

We made our camp below, we had a dog and a few willows to cook him. I could hear Colter consoling himself. I did the same.

Oct. 13, '05.

Towards evening we came to a very rocky place, the River is all confined in a narrow channel about 15 yards wide and swift as a mill tale, the canoes run down this Channel swifter than any horse could ever run. This is much the fastest I have ever gone it is indeed so fast as a human being will ever travel, it is exhilarating in the extreme, me and Colter were whooping and shouting.

Oct. 14, '05.

At noon we came to a very bad rapid, Twisted Hair had warned us. Three of the canoes ran fast on a rock, two on at a time, they were in great danger of being lost. Sgt. Ordway's canoe was in the worst shape, the men got out on the rock and attempted to shove her off but waves dashed over her bow so that they could not.

Colter and I stemmed the swift current, we took off considerable of her baggage. The canoe then broke away from them and left four men, Ordway, the Fields brothers, and Shields standing on the rock. The water was to their knees, it ran swift over the Smooth rock. They were in great danger, Colter and I unloaded the wet baggage and set out for them, we managed to rescue them. Our loss was, however, very great, we lost some bedding, tomahawks, shot pouches, skins, & etc.

and all the roots we have managed to purchase which had been set aside for emergencies.

In a day, Twisted Hair informs, we will come to the Columbia River, where a different nation from the Nez Perce lives. He can no longer interpret or guide us and will be returning to his village. We will then be on our own in a country where not a man among us, nor Sacajawea either, can speak one word of the native language and, until we get to the mouth of the river, no white man has ever yet been seen.

Fortunately, we find that Sacajawea reconciles all the Indians as to our friendly intentions. A woman with a Party of men is a token of peace.

DESCENDING THE COLUMBIA

Oct. 16, '05.

We set off early, past some rapids, and in the after part of the day came in site of the great Columbia River, which comes in from the north. This is a broad and beautiful river, its waters perfectly Clear, we see to the bottom even at 20 feet of depth. The country around is one continued plain that is barren, not a tree to be seen. We made camp on the point between the two rivers.

There is an immense number of dead salmon on this river, on the shores or floating on the water. Some Indians come in signing, they signed that they was friendly. These natives sold us seven dogs, the Capts. warned us not to use them.

Oct. 17, '05.

Capt. C. had Colter and me take him in our little canoe up the Columbia, we ascended it ten miles. There was great numbers of Indians on the banks viewing us and 18 canoes accompanying us. We came to at a village which was of Mat lodges, this village was crowded with men, women, and children, there was many squaws engaged in splitting and drying salmon.

These squaws are fat, of low stature, broad faces, heads flattened from childhood, with the forehead compressed so as to form a straight line from the nose to the crown of the head. These People who are middle-aged, have lost their teeth, the method they have of using the dried salmon, which is merely worming it and eating the rind and scales with the flesh of the Fish, no doubt contributes to those bad teeth.

Those people appear to live in a state of comparative Happiness, certain that they do not have to work as the natives of the plains and mountains must work to obtain sustenance, they have but to pick up the fish from the shore and dry them on their Scaffolds. The populations of these people are truly astonishing to us, not even the Mandans are so numerous.

Oct. 18, '05.

In the after part of the day we set off on the Columbia for the ocean, the river is near a mile wide, Smooth and pleasant, the country around barren and level. Great numbers of Indians on the banks, immense quantities of salmon drying on the Scaffolds.

I have a game I play with Pomp, I grasp him under his arms and toss him so high in the air as I can, I catch him as he comes down. He screams in Pleasure, whenever he sees me he holds up his arms for another toss. Sacajawea indicated that Peme's time has come, I am by now a Father, she says. It is frustrating in the extreme not to know if the Baby is a boy or a girl. I hope a boy.

I think of Peme whenever I play with Pomp, today I held his hands and whirled in a circle. Capt. C. admonished me to be careful but Sacajawea smiled and

Pomp laughed, Capt. C. supposed it was alright.

Pomp grabs my beard and pulls, when I yell he laughs and pulls harder. Oh how I hope I have a son.

Oct. 21, '05.

The current was confined in a narrow channel, the standing waves were immense, near six feet high, well over our heads. They were broken by a group of huge rocks, there were eddies and swirls, our Canoe was half filled with water but there was no chance to pull to shore to empty her, we could but barely maneuver. I was afraid for my life, this was stark terror.

We picked our way through those Rocks the best we could, I was sure we was goners, suddenly there was a rock, near submerged, straight in front of us, Colter called out, Left, and started to pull her left from his place in the Bow just as I called out, Right, and back paddled on my side, we turned Broadside and hit that rock square in the middle, we were both thrown over.

Colter hit his head on the rock, he was near drowned. I tried to grab him as I swept down the Stream, but could not catch him, the current was too strong. York coming up in the canoe which was following did catch Colter by the back of his shirt and hauled him into his canoe. I swam to shore, York's Canoe pulled over and set Colter ashore and set off again to rescue our canoe.

Colter had recovered. He came up to me furious and red in the face, he was enraged.

You son of a Bitch, he shouted, I told you Left.

Go to Hell, I replied, I told you Right.

He pitched into me, I was surprised and he got me down. He began beating my Head on the ground, he had a hold of my hair. I got a hand under his chin and threw him back, I wrapped my left arm around his Neck and stuck my right thumb into his eye socket, I informed him if he did not admit Enough it would cost him his eye.

Enough, he said, I let go and turned to help Capt. C. and his Party unload our Canoe which they had brought ashore. Colter grabbed my shoulder and spun me around, he fetched me a tremendous kick in my parts, the pain was too incredible to describe, I fell to the ground clutching my parts. I was scarcely able to see. Colter commenced kicking at me again, I heard Capt. C. shout at him to Stop.

He did not stop, he was insensible with Rage, I could not defend myself, I was in too great of pain. York came up behind Colter, he grabbed him by the back of his Shirt and pulled him off.

Let go you damn nigger, Colter shouted, and commenced to kick York.

York wrapped his big hand around Colter's neck, lifted him clean off the ground with one hand, and shook him like a dog. Now listen White boy, York said, his voice was low but very intense, just listen. You ever try to kick me again you are a dead man.

Colter was astonished, his eyes near bulged from his Head. York tossed him aside, he fell to the ground, when he pulled himself up he turned to Capt. C. to ask if he allowed a damn nigger to talk to a white man like that.

Capt. C. smiled. Colter, he said, you should know that York don't like it when someone fails to obey my orders. I told you to Stop and you should have stopped.

Drewyer came to me just as I finished writing, he

said I should not blame Colter, we were taking tremendous risks in running these rapids and spills were bound to happen, that tempers were short throughout the Party as a consequence of these risks and due to our diet which is insufficient to sustain men that are laboring so hard as we.

But kicking a man in his parts has no excuse, I said.

Drewyer responded that I must remember Colter grew up fighting that way, it was natural to him. Besides, he said, you came damn close to gouging out Colter's eye, there is no excuse for that either.

He started it, I thought to myself, but did not say aloud. Then, I wondered, Would I really have torn his eye out? I am ashamed even to think it, just the idea of it is barbaric. But I fear I would have done it, I was that enraged. I fear, too, I am becoming as wild as this river. I do not like this about myself, I am fast becoming a violent man, this is not right.

Oct. 24, '05.

This morning we came to a bad rapid, we scouted for a portage but huge rocks and cliffs on the banks made this near impossible. Capt. C. determined to pass through despite the horrid appearance of this agitated gut swelling, boiling and whirling water in every direction. We were all afraid, but Cruzzate reckoned that by good Steering we could pass down safe.

I was in the Indian canoe with Drewyer, York, Capt. C. and Sacajawea, who had Pomp in the cradleboard on her back. As our canoe was the best calculated to make this run we led the way, the Indians were gathered at the foot of the rapids, they were waiting for us to Perish, they intended to enrich themselves with our baggage, & etc.

To the astonishment of all those Indians we passed through safe. Pomp is delighted to make these runs, he laughs and cries out in joy as we speed along and the water splashes in his Face.

Oct. 25, '05.

We run more rapids today, the men who can not swim portaged around with our most valuable articles. We made it Safe, to the amazement of the Indians who were observing, notwithstanding that at one place the River was confined in a narrow channel of 25 yards only, high rocks on each Side, the current very rapid and full of whirlpools. We ran down very fast, Pomp was all smiles and laughs.

Oct. 28, '05.

Set out early, at five miles we came to at a village, the People friendly. One of the warriors showed us some of his war implements, he had some English the only word we could make out was "good." This warrior took his medicine bag and opened it, he showed us 14 fingers, these were the fingers of his enemies he had killed in war. He harangued us, bragging of what he had done in war.

From this spot we can see the mountains first seen by the British traders who come to the mouth of this river, Mt. Hood as the British called it is South, its top covered with snow.

Oct. 31, '05.

This after I shot a geese which was flying, it was a good shot, I was pleased, the geese fell into the River above the Shute, I figured him for lost. But an Indian on the bank plunged, to my great astonishment and fright, into the River and swam to the goose, there was great danger, the rapids are bad, the current dashed amongst the Rocks, had the Indian got sucked in he was lost for certain, but he got the goose and managed to get it to shore just above the Suck.

I suffered this Indian to keep the goose, which he had so richly earned, he about half picked it and Spited it up with the guts in it to roast.

These Indians are remarkable, some of the things they can do on this river sets us back considerably. We have an advantage on them, however, we run these rapids which they never do, but then we are in a hurry, so anxious is the Entire Party to see the ocean, Indians are never in a hurry. I anticipate Capt. C. will have us past these rapids once we have gotten past the Great Shute.

Nov. 2, '05.

This after we passed a high detached rock which stands in a Bottom on the starboard side, it is near 800 feet high and 400 paces around, Capt. C. names it Beacon Rock. The river near a mile wide, we made 29 miles today from the Great Shute.

Nov. 3, '05.

The fog detained us until 10 o'clock when we proceeded on. The river is slow and tidal, the Country about low, rich and thickly timbered on each Side, immense numbers of fowls flying in every direction, such as Swan, geese, Brants, Cranes, Storks, white gulls, cormorants, plovers, and etc.

We camped on a large island in the middle of the river which Capt. C. calls Diamond Island from its appearance. In the distance, far back to the SE, there is an immensely high round mountain. The first is named by the British Mt. Hood, the second Mt. Rainy. Made 13 miles.

Some Indians come over, Capt. Lewis borrowed a small Canoe of those Indians and asked who wanted to go fowl hunting. I jumped up and grabbed my gun as did the Fields brothers, Frasier and Colter. But when Colter saw me he sat down again, he said never mind.

We carried the Canoe to a Lake in the middle of the Island where Fowls covered the water, it was a beautiful sight. Our shots rang out over the constant honking and quacking of the birds. The sky filled with birds, enough to cut off the moon, we came near to oversetting the Canoe. When the fowl settled back down, we did a repeat, and in short order we had three geese, 3 Swan, 8 brant, and 5 ducks, which Capt. Lewis allowed was enough.

It made a most sumptuous supper, all are contented, we are past the rapids, the Ocean must be just around the next bend or the one after that, these are high times.

Nov. 4, '05.

We made camp on the starboard side, some Indians from above came down to visit and trade, they had a large canoe which was ornamented with Images carved in wood, there was a Bear in front and a warrior in the stern, painted and fixed neatly on the Canoe, which rose to near the height of a man. These Indians had on their finery viz. scarlet and blue blankets, Sailor Jackets, overalls, shirts and hats, & etc., all of which they obtain from the traders that come to this River's mouth. One of them could curse some words in English.

Capt. C. passed his tomahawk pipe and the Indians all smoked, meanwhile we sat to our dinner, Capt. C.

permitted the Indians to continue smoking.

Suddenly Capt. C. noticed that his pipe was missing, this is perhaps his most valuable article, he jumped to his feet and strode to the Indian circle and immediately set to searching those Indians, but failed to find his pipe. He marched to their canoe and searched it and found nothing.

We were all watching him throwing things and cursing, while we were watching one of those Indians steal Charbono's great coat. We all commenced to search as Charbono called to Mon Dew for help, we found the coat stuffed under the root of a tree but not the pipe.

Capt. C. was much displeased with those assuming and disagreeable fellows, he chased them out of our camp.

Nov. 6, '05.

We made camp under a high hill opposite to a large Rock, it was with difficulty that we found a place out of the ranch of the Tide and level enough to make a camp. We made 34 miles today.

Notwithstanding our disagreeable Situation, hemmed

into this small cove as we are, all joy broke loose when Capt. C. called out, Ocean in View! We all scrambled on the rocks to see, we could not see much for the fog and the rain, but we could hear the breakers roaring on the Rocky Shores.

Drewyer commenced to do an Indian war dance, we all joined in, Rubin Fields beat on a canoe to imitate the sound of a drum. Cruzzate brought out his fiddle and York danced, we all danced.

Capt. C. and Capt. Lewis solemnly shook hands, we all cheered at this. Then they placed their arms around one another and hugged, we cheered again. We all shook hands, every man with every man and all with the Capts.

Tonight, despite the rain and fog we sat at a fire and talked until past midnight. Mainly we were bragging on ourselves. We agreed that we were the first white men to come by land to this place.

York allowed as how he was the first slave and wondered, did this mean he would be famous? We all assured him that he would. Sacajawea too, Capt. C. said, and Pomp.

I am so proud to be a member of the Corps of Discovery, I wish my mother and father were here to see. When I left home to join this Expedition, my father said we should never make it to the Pacific Ocean. I should like to show him that he was Wrong as usual.

I wish too that Peme and my Baby were here to celebrate with us.

Colter wished he had some whiskey, that it would make a perfect evening more perfect.

EXPLORING THE SEACOAST

Nov. 8, '05.

Rain all day. We set out at 9 o'clock. The river is near seven miles wide, at 3 miles we come to a Bay which is on the starboard side, we were fortunate we caught the falling tide and rode it to the west point of the Bay. When we rounded that point we discovered that the Swells or Waves were so high that it was imprudent to proceed, we drew up the canoes and made Camp.

Our situation is miserable, we have not sufficient level land to lie on, the high Hills behind jutting in so close and steep we cannot retreat inland, the water on the river too Salt for use, it is near impossible to keep a fire going in this constant rain, fleas cover our clothes and Bodies, the waves at such a height we cannot move from this place.

We are extremely anxious to discover some white men on Ships in this vicinity, we can stock up on trade goods, get some whiskey and tobacco, learn the news from the U. States, and provide copies of the Capts. papers, observations and journals so as to ensure their safe arrival in Washington.

Nov. 9, '05.

We could not proceed today the Waves were too high. Rained hard all day. This after the tide came in so strong with high Waves it covered our camp, it was only with the greatest exertion on our part that we avoided losing our canoes, which all filled and which were in great danger of being crushed by immense logs that came crashing in.

One of these monsters was riding a wave, it was headed straight for a Canoe, York leaped forward, he was in water past his waist, he caught the log and held it, he is the strongest man alive I believe.

When the tide ran out we measured that log. It was

200 feet long and 7 feet in diameter. Where can trees of this size grow, we wonder.

Nov. 10, '05.

Nothing to eat tonight but dried fish pounded, this is insufficient. Notwithstanding our sad situation, the men are cheerful and anxious to explore more of this shoreline and to find white men in ships.

Nov. 11, '05.

It blew a storm all day, we were stuck. At noon five Indians came across from the larboard shore, near six miles distant in a small Canoe. They came through the highest waves we ever saw a small Canoe ride, tremendous waves breaking with great violence against the Shores, rain falling in torrents, many times they were out of sight between the waves, Capt. C. said those Indians were certainly the best Canoe navigators he ever saw.

Nov. 12, '05.

A repeat of yesterday except that at noon the heavens darkened, a storm succeeded which raised the seas tremendously, breaking with great force and fury against the rocks and trees on which we lie, our situation was seriously dangerous.

When the storm fell off and the tide began to recede, Capt. C. walked amongst the litter and debris that once was our baggage, he allowed how it would be distressing to a feeling person to see our Situation at this time.

Nov. 13, '05.

Capt. C. directed me, Willard and Colter to attempt to get around the point in the Indian Canoe to examine the River and the Bay below for a good harbor for our Canoe and a Satisfactory campsite and look for the ships and the camps of white men that the Indians said were there.

We set off, our hearts were pounding near as strong as the waves, we near overset twice, but we soon learned to turn her into the wave as it approached, then paddle in the trough to proceed. We got around the point. We found no white People, no Bay, no Camp.

At three miles we found a good Canoe harbor, there

were two camps of Indians there. We signed with these Indians the best we could but could only learn little. We asked where was the camp of the white men, they indicated there was none. I wonder did those Indians above lie to us?

Nov. 14, '05.

This morning at first light the Indians were gone, so was Colter's knife and knapsack containing all his articles. It was a good thing we slept with our rifles beside us under our robes. Colter was angry, he swore to catch those bastards.

We found nothing to report, we made a camp in a niche where five Indian warriors joined us. We agree to divide the watch and sleep with our rifles under our heads.

Nov. 15, '05.

I was awaken by Willard's calling out, You Son of a Bitch, Give Back my Gun! He was wrestling with an Indian for it, one of the other fellows came up and held Willard's arm while the other ran off with the rifle.

I reached for my rifle, it was gone.

I ran to Willard and kicked the fellow holding him who ran to his party which was waving our rifles in the air and dancing and whooping. Fortunate for us they did not know the workings of those rifles, we pitched into them, I fetched the warrior with my rifle a kick in his parts, he doubled over, but just as I near had the Rifle in my grasp another of those damn Rascals kicked me, I fell over the Indian I had kicked.

Willard had been knocked down too, he was beside me. Those Indians pulled their knives and began threatening gestures, & etc. I took out Mr. Boone's knife and thought, You have killed Indians before knife, now get ready to do it again. Willard pulled his knife, the Indians prepared to pitch into us, all five of them. I was afraid but excited, I wanted to plunge the knife into the guts of one of those Indians.

Just at that instant, there was a shot that rang out, we, all of us, Willard and me and the Indians looked over, there was Capt. Lewis, Drewyer and the Fields brothers standing there, their rifles aimed at the Indians. Those Indians dropped our rifles and ran off.

We were overjoyed to see Capt. Lewis and Party, they related that yesterday Colter had returned to camp just as the Indians who had robbed him arrived by Canoe, that Colter had treated those People very roughly and retrieved his knife and articles, that Capt. Lewis had then set out overland to search for us.

Capt. C. and Party was in their Camp, he announced this was as far as the canoes would proceed, beyond is too dangerous. He estimates that we have come from Camp Wood 4,133 miles, that 379 miles of this was over mountains by foot. From this place we can see Cape Disappointment and Point Adams as the British name them, beyond is the open ocean.

Five Indians come up, these Indians are called Chinooks, but we think they are devils, rascals, and thieves. Capt. C. told those People that if any of their nation stole anything that the Sentinel would most certainly shoot them.

Tonight I am concerned about myself, I would have killed those Indians so easy as I kill a deer, the truth is I wanted to kill, it was my wish to plunge my knife into the heart of one of those devils and feel the blood cover my hand. This is not like me.

Nov. 20, '05.

One of these Indians had on a robe made of two sea otter skins. Clothes are scarce with us, we are all near naked, the Capts.' leather jackets are worn and rotten, the Capts. wanted that robe, which was indeed more beautiful than any fur any of us had yet seen. Capt. Lewis offered a Blanket, a red military Coat, and many other articles, the Indian refused all. Capt. C. stepped forward, he wanted that fur even worse than Capt. Lewis, he offered near everything he had to trade, the Indian refused.

That Indian kept pointing to Sacajawea and her blue belt, which is the envy of every Indian from Mandan Village to the Pacific Ocean, it is indeed handsome. Sacajawea watched Capt. C. attempting to trade for a long while, finally she stepped forward and handed the Indian her blue Belt and he gave her the robe, which she instantly handed to Capt. C. He was well satisfied.

As this belt was the most valuable article in the possession of the Party, Charbono was much put out that his wife gave it away for nothing in return for him or her. I informed him that we all get the benefit, that a happy Capt. C. makes for a happy Party.

I traded with one of those Indians, I gave him an old razor I no longer use as I never shave my face, I am proud of my beard, which Colter assures is indeed handsome. I bought a hat made of the bark of white cedar and bear grass, it is very handsomely wrought and keeps off the rain, it is conical. Sacajawea laughs to see me in it. I cued my hair like Capt. C. and let it hang over my shoulders. When Pomp saw me he laughed and clapped his hands and pulled on my pig tails.

Nov. 24, '05.

Capt. Lewis asked each in turn to vote, for my part I voted to cross and examine and then move up to the Falls if the Situation on the opposite Shore is not satisfactory. Five voted to go to the Falls, the others to cross and examine.

Nov. 25, '05.

Agreeable to the vote of yesterday, this morning we packed and set off up the river to get to a narrower part where we can cross in our Canoes. We got so far as our campsite of Nov. 7 and made Camp.

Dec. 3, '05.

We have found a site suitable for our winter Quarters, 3 miles up a small river on a point of high land, and plenty of Timber and fresh water springs, with elk in sufficient numbers for our sustenance.

Dec. 8, '05.

The Party has been felling trees for a Fort and huts these past days. All pitching in with a will so as to get a roof for some relief from this constant rain. This is more wet weather than any of us have ever seen, we make a joke about the Pacific Ocean, there has not been one Pacific Day since our arrival here one month past.

Dec. 9, '05.

This morning Capt. C. picked his two best hunters, Drewyer and me, and sent us after the gang of Elk. It took the better part of the morning to cross the Bog, when we got to the rise we saw the gang moving slowly through open timber. We circled and snuck close and fired together and each killed an Elk, before they had all run off. Drewyer had loaded again and shot another, I was not so fast.

We brought the meat and skins and found Capt. C. and Party at a small Indian Village of 3 houses and 12 families. Their houses are sunk into the ground about 4 feet, the walls, roof and gable ends are of Split pine boards, the doors small, with a ladder to descent to the inner part, the fires are in the middle.

These are an extraordinary People, these are the Clatsop Nation. They are much neater in their diet than Indians are commonly, they frequently wash their hands and face. These Indians gave us a meal of dried berries as a kind of syrup which was pleasant, we ate Cockle shells and a kind of soup made of berries mixed with roots, we brought Elk meat, it was a sumptuous feast.

WINTER AT FORT CLATSOP

Dec. 10, '05.

We returned to the Party which was engaged in felling trees for our huts. Pat Gass is well satisfied with these trees.

Thus, our winter home shall be of the straightest and most beautiful logs, these are Balsam Pine. We are Situated some seven miles from the Sea Coast, five of those miles through thick woods with ravines, hills and Swamps.

This is prime hunting country, the Elk cannot be compared to the buffalo as meat and shooting an Elk in the woods cannot be compared to riding beside a stampede of buffalo snorting, bellowing, running near as fast as the best horse, tossing up their horns to catch your horse, but so far as hunting goes, the Elk are the greater challenge, you must use all your skills and not just your Daring, you must finds the game, and Circle, and sneak up, taking into account the Wind, the lay of the land, the probable movements of the quarry, depends in large Measure on the time of the season and the time of the day and whether or not this gangue has been hunted recently, and much more.

I am in short excited by the prospect of a winter of hunting the Elk. In the past month each time the Capts. tell Drewyer to select a man to join him in the hunt, he has picked me, a singular honor and today confirmed by Capt. C. as permanent, I shall be Drewyer's partner as hunters for the Party.

I am overjoyed and full of sinful pride that I cannot let go. Near every man of this Party grew up on the Frontier, they all of them were hunters and woodsmen before they became soldiers, they are young and fit and eager, Each of them would like to be Drewyer's companion as hunting is fun and all else is work. Yet I got the Place!

Dec. 12, '05.

By evening I had drug in four more Elk, Drewyer had eight, altogether we killed 18 Elk today. We hung them around the meadow and made our Camp, we ate tongue and marrow bones and sat by the fire. Drewyer remarked that this was the greatest day of hunting of his life. He said he couldn't ask for a better partner either.

I am proud and happy, if it could be with Drewyer, I think I could spend the remainder of my life as a hunter.

Dec. 16, '05.

A dreadful night of rain, we sat up the whole night under Elk skins, wet and cold without fire or shelter, our appearance is truly distressing. There were tremendous gusts of winds, trees falling in every direction, whirlwinds, Hail and Thunder, this weather continued all day. Capt. C. declared that this Certainly was one of the worst days that ever was.

Dec. 25, '05.

Our feast on this day of the nativity of Christ was as follows, poor Elk, so much spoiled that we ate it through mere necessity, and we are without salt to season it, and nothing but pure water to drink.

Jan'y 1, '06.

We woke the Capts. at dawn with a volley and shouts of Happy New Year. Drewyer and I went hunting, we brought back two Elk, we gave the marrow bone and tongue to the Capts., which they appreciated much.

Capt. Lewis was cheerful today which is a relief, he has been gloomy and sad since we crossed the mountains, he smiled at us, he said, Well at least this is a better repast than that of Christmas Day. He said he could now look forward in the anticipation of the next New Year Day in mirth and hilarity in the bosom of his family, with zest to the event given by recollections of the present misery.

Tonight he writes in his journal for the first time in some months, it appears that the thought that we will be back in the U. States this year has revived his spirits.

❧

Jan'y 7, '06.

Capt. C. and some of the Party come to the shore today, they have come to see the beached whale and obtain some blubber if possible.

Sacajawea was with them, York told me that Capt. C. did not wish her to come, he did not want Pomp to be near the Salt water which he says is unhealthy, he is more protective of Pomp each day. But Sacajawea was very insistant to be permitted to go, she told Capt. C. firmly that she had traveled a long way with us to see the great ocean waters, and had not yet been permitted to go to the ocean, and now that the monster fish was also to be seen, she thought it very hard she could not be allowed to accompany the Party. Capt. C. thereupon suffered her to come on.

Jan'y 8, '06.

I guided Capt. C. and Party over the cliffs and rocks to the Kilamox Nation near the whale. We found only the skeleton of this Monster on the Sand. This skeleton measured 105 feet, the head alone measured 12 feet.

Sacajawea remarked that no one at Mandan Village would ever believe that such a fish could be, she thought the whole voyage worth the while just to see this curiosity. Capt. C. attempted to explain to her the story of Jonah and the whale, though she has become a great believer in the great medicine our God can do, she could not believe about Jonah.

Jan'y 27, '06.

I have killed 13 Elk this week, more than a sufficiency, but in place of thanks from the Party for my exertions, what I get is curses and complaints about the inferior quality of the meat in these indifferent Elk.

Clatsops come to the Fort often, led by their Chief, Comowooll. The squaws come with them to sell their favors, but few indulge. These squaws are dirty and naked wretches. They are a disgusting sight. Even Colter will not touch them, Goodrich and McNeal did indulge, as a consequence they have the Louis Veneri. Capt. Lewis treats them with the mercury.

Jan'y 28, '06.

All are hungry all the time, despite a sufficiency of Elk. But this flesh of lean Elk boiled with pure water and but a dash of salt does not satisfy. We have long since used up the whale blubber despite that we used it very sparingly.

All have keen appetites, Capt. Lewis frequently inquires of Charbono, the cook, whether dinner or breakfast is ready. But all complain when they eat the Elk and complain after that they are not full.

Feb. 1, '06.

Comowooll and some of his warriors came on today in their canoes. These canoes are remarkably neat, light, and well adapted for riding high waves. They ride the waves in these Canoes with safety and apparently without concern where we should have thought it impossible for any vessel of the same size to live a moment.

These canoes are built of white cedar or the fir. They are cut out of a solid stick of timber, the gunwales fold over outwards forming a rim to prevent the water coming into the canoe. The large canoes are upwards of 50 feet long and will carry 5 tons or from 20 to 30 persons, they are waxed and painted and ornamented with curious images at bow and stern, these images rise to the height of five feet.

I cannot agree with Capt. Lewis that the Indians are savages. Some of them are to be sure, certain it is that the Sioux are Savages and these Indians of the Coast are near as bad except not so warlike, and by all accounts the Blackfeet are the worst of all, but this does not mean all Indians are savages.

Sacajawea is not a savage.

The Nez Perce are not savages, they fed us when we were starved, they nursed us when we were sick, they guided us, they are caring for our horses through the winter, there is no doubt in my mind that we would never have got here without them.

The Shoshones are not savages, indeed they are gentlemen who are true to their word. Cameahwait cuts a fine figure, he is a leader. Even though his People were near starving, he postponed the excursion to the buffalo country so as to bring us over the Divide. He taught us the geography of the Region, he sold us horses at the best Price we have seen west of St. Louis, he provided Old Toby to guide us, he was a delightful host. Without

Cameahwait and his People, we would never have got here.

We talked tonight about what we would do when we get back, we are counting the days until we start (it is 58 days), most said they would take up their farms in the Missouri Valley, some said they would stay in the Army, that they liked the Army life. Charbono said he intended to stay with the Mandans.

Colter said none of that was for him, that he has never seen such country as the Missouri nor such mountains as the Rockies, had never dreamed such could Exist, so as for him he had found his Place and he intended to return to the wilderness so soon as he was discharged in St. Louis, to remain in paradise for the remainder of his days.

Feb. 11, '06.

Today is Pomp's first birthday, we celebrated the best we could, we sang songs to him. He moves around the fire, holding first this man's Leg then that one's, he pokes with his fingers, he picks up sticks or knives or whatever lays around and Examines it careful, often he throws things or puts them in his Mouth, his mother never corrects him, she explains that it is wrong to correct a Boy. We all indulge him.

Feb. 24, '06.

I spend the day hunting, I saw neither Elk nor deer. Drewyer says we have pretty well eliminated the Elk population of this neighborhood, we will have to go further for our meat.

Tonight Comowooll and 12 of his people come for a visit, they brought a sea otter skin, some hats and a species of small fish which now begins to run and which the Clatsops take in great quantities in the Columbia River.

This fish is the Candle fish, it is excellent and most welcome. Comowooll taught us how to prepare it, which is by roasting a number of these fish together on a wooden spit without any previous preparation whatsoever. They are so fat they require no additional sauce, and I think them superior to any fish I ever tasted. The bones are so soft and fine that they form no obstruction in eating this fish.

March 2, '06.

We brought in six Elk, we now have provisions for a week. Late this evening Drewyer returned with a most acceptable supply of fat Sturgeon, fresh Anchovies, and a bushel of Wappetoe root, which he purchased from the Indians.

We cook the sturgeon in the Indian Way, which is to build a brisk fire, then lay a parcel of stones on it. When the stones are hot they are arranged so as to form a tolerable level surface, the sturgeon which is cut into large fillets is now laid on the hot stones, a parcel of small boughs laid on the sturgeon, then a second course of sturgeon, then more boughs, thus repeating alternate layers. This is covered closed with mats. Water is then poured in such manner as to run in among the hot stones which produces a vapor which is confined by the mats and thus cooks the fish. Sturgeon thus cooked is much superior to either boiled or roasted.

March 23, '06.

Despite that it continues to rain and blow, Capt. Lewis said we must get away from here, we decide that though the wind is pretty high we can pass Point William.

We arranged the baggage and at 1 o'clock we bid a final adieu to Fort Clatsop. The best that can be said of it is that we lived through it.

We made it past Point William and at 6 o'clock made Camp at the mouth of a small creek. Drewyer who had gone ahead by land had killed two Elk.

We made 16 miles today.

We have begun the journey back to our homes and loved ones. Where are mine, I wonder, at Mandan Village or in the U. States?

ASCENDING THE COLUMBIA

March 24, '06.

We paddled up river today, we got amongst the Seal Islands and mistook our route, a Clatsop observing pursued and overtook us and put us in the right channel. This Indian then saw the Canoe which we had stolen from his People, he claimed it. Capt. Lewis offered him an Elk's skin for the canoe, he took it and returned.

Capt. Lewis then told me I could stop being so disapproving about the theft of the Canoe, that it now had been paid for. I was disgusted, I told him he knew that the Canoe was worth 50 Elk skins, that the crime had been but compounded, then I slunk off. Colter come to me, he said, George you know we could not start back without that canoe, we had no choice but to take it.

We did, I insisted, we could pay with a kittle.

You know the Capts. will never part with any of our camp gear, Colter persisted.

We do not need these kittles, I said, we have more guns than we need, we have far more powder and lead and tomahawks & etc. then we need, We could have paid.

Baby, he called me.

Thief, I called him.

March 25, '06.

We set out at 7 o'clock and continue our route along the South Coast of the river, the wind against us and a strong current, our progress was but slow. We came to at an Indian camp, Capt. C. pronounced it the dirtiest stinkingest place he ever saw in any shape whatever. These people gave us some Seal to eat which was a great improvement to poor Elk.

March 28, '06.

The Skillutes having informed that there was game in this neighborhood, the Capts. sent Drewyer and me and four others out hunting this morning. I killed two deer, altogether we got seven. We brought in three of those deer, we returned for the remainder only to find that the Eagles and Vultures had devoured the meat. One of those Vultures had dragged a large buck 30 yards, skinned it, and broken the back bone. Fortunately Drewyer came in late with the Fields brothers, they had three deer, a goose, some ducks, and a tiger cat Drewyer had killed.

March 30, '06.

We made progress but slowly today as Seaman explored the shores, one of the reasons being hundreds of natives came out to see us, we were surrounded much of the time by Canoes, they slow us considerably. Their principal object was merely to indulge their curiosity in looking at us.

Capt. Lewis discovered a mountain to the SE covered with snow, he names it Mt. Jefferson.

April 2, '06.

We remain encamped whilst we attempt to purchase enough dried fish and roots to sustain us on this river, where all the natives are near starving, they wait for the Salmon to begin to run. Capt. C. has meanwhile taken Colter and some others to explore a river we failed to notice coming down last fall, as it was hid by a large island, this river is called by the Indians the Mult-no-Mah.

April 11, '06.

We have come to the Falls of the Columbia, we spent the day portaging the baggage and hauling the Canoes up the rapids by the means of chords, this is immensely laborious work.

Tonight three Indians stole Capt. Lewis's dog Seaman, which is near as big a colt and much finer than the Indian dogs and a great pet of all the Party, Capt. Lewis was furious. He sent me, Drewyer, and Colter in pursuit of the thieves, he told us if they made the least resistance or difficulty to fire on them.

We tracked the thieves, we found them at a Distance of 2 miles, we made to shoot them and they let the dog go.

Others of these people tried to steal an axe, the sentinel who was Goodrich stopped them, the Capts. informed them by Signs that if they made any further attempts to steal our property we should put them to an instant Death.

For my part I would do so only with great reluctance, I should hate to kill a man for a dog or an axe, but Colter and Drewyer and the most of the others had their blood up, they are well disposed to kill some of these red devils.

Their chief was mortified at the conduct of his People, he explained that there were a few very bad men among them, that these had been the principal actors in this scene of outrage.

I reminded Colter, who was ranting and raving about killing those thieves, that we had stolen a Canoe from the Indians. He said that was different, I don't see how.

April 16, '06.

After three days of tremendous toil the Capts. have yielded tour entreaties and decided to go hereafter by land to the Nez Perce. To that end we have brought the baggage to a Skillute Village above the long narrows and made all preparations for trade with these Indians for horses. The Chief gave us onions to eat.

After we ate Capt. C. attempted to trade, these People asked nearly half of the merchandize we have with us for one horse only, a price we could not think of giving.

We put aside the trading, at the native's request Cruzzate brought out his fiddle. York, Sacajawea, and me led a Virginy Reel which delighted the natives.

This is the great mart of all this country, ten different tribes come here to trade, as a consequence these People are hagglers. The Skillutes have cloth, knives, axes, and beads which they bargain for horses, buffalo robes, and such articles with Indians from so far away as the Rocky Mountains.

We sleep tonight in the lodges, fleas and mice make sleep impossible.

April 17, '06.
Capt. C. bargained all day, the Skillutes sold him three horses, but came back later and demanded more for them, when he would not yield they took back their

horses. Charbono purchased a very fine mare for which he gave Ermine skin, Elk teeth, a belt, and some other articles, all of which was Sacajawea's property. She offered it freely, she said she did not want old Charbono to have to carry his baggage on his back.

April 18, '06.

One of the Chiefs had a wife who was afflicted with pains in her back. Capt. C. told us that though she was a sulky Bitch this was a good opportunity to get her on our Side, he rubbed camphor on her temples and back and applied worm flannel to her back, this restored her, she was grateful. Her husband, the Chief, then traded for two horses, Capt. Lewis gave over one of our large Kittles for those horses.

We offered to trade two of our canoes to those People, they knowing that we no longer needed them and would be leaving them behind refused to trade. Capt. Lewis damned them and ordered the Fields brothers to cut up those canoes for fire wood, very much to the disappointment of the Indians.

April 19, '06.

The Capts. traded two of our kittles today to acquire four additional horses, we now have only one small kittle for each mess of 8 men.

Capt. Lewis is near beside himself with rage at those Indians for the prices they charge for indifferent horses, he lost his temper with Willard who was negligent in his attention to a horse under his charge and suffered it to wander off, Capt. Lewis reprimanded him severely for this piece of negligence, he swore at Willard which is not like him.

The Indians celebrated last night, there was great joy among them in the consequence of the arrival of the salmon. One salmon was caught, this is the harbinger of good news, the Indians informed that these fish would arrive in great quantities in the course of about five days.

April 20, '06.

The natives pilfered six tomahawks and a knife last night. Capt. Lewis spoke to the Chief with some heat, the chief was angry with his people and harangued them but nothing was returned. Capt. Lewis was further provoked when a horse he had purchased yesterday could not be found, the chief informed him that the Horse had been gambled away previously by the rascal who had sold it to him and had been taken away by a man of another nation who had won it. Capt. Lewis took back the goods he had used to pay for the horse—skins, old irons, and a canoe for its beads. The smallest canoe, for which the Indians would offer but a pittance, he ordered cut up for firewood.

April 21, '06.

A cold morning. An Indian stole a tomahawk last night, we searched many of them but failed to find it. Capt. Lewis ordered all the spare poles, paddles, and the balance of our canoe on the Fire. He said, Do not leave a particle for these thieves. When he saw a fellow stealing an iron socket from a canoe pole he exploded like Mt. Vesuvius, he called, Damn You! And hit the fellow aside the head, the Indian fell and Capt. Lewis proceeded to kick him severe Blows.

He then directed the Fields brothers to pick the fellow up and kick him out of camp, which they did. Capt.

Lewis then informed the Indians that he would shoot to kill the first of them that attempted to steal anything. He said we were not afraid to fight them, that he could kill them all right now if he wished, and set fire to their houses, but that it was not his wish to treat them with severity if they would let our property be. The chiefs who were present hung their heads and said nothing.

These people certainly are villains, they steal and lie as natural as they breathe. Still it discomforts me to hear Capt. Lewis threaten to kill them and burn their houses for such little things, or beat one of them for taking an old socket. But notwithstanding that Capt. Lewis reacted with more severity than necessary, I find myself discomforted also by the thought of living amongst the Indians. Then I look at Sacajawea, who is playing a hand clapping game with Pomp as I write, and my heart beats yearning for Peme. I remind myself that not all Indians are bad.

April 22, '06.

We set out at 7 o'clock, all on foot, near half the men leading horses that carry our baggage. At the top of a hill Charbono's horse broke away, threw his load and plunged full speed down the hill into a village. Charbono went down to retrieve the horse and baggage, when he came back he reported that these Indians had stolen a robe that had fallen off.

Capt. Lewis announced that he was determined either to make those Indians deliver the robe or burn their houses. He added that he would gladly kill them all except that their defenseless state pleads forgiveness so far as respects their lives.

We descended to that village prepared for war, when it was clear to the Indians that we were ready to burn their houses they produced the robe, we proceeded on.

April 28, '06.

At first light the Great Chief Yellept of the Walla Walla Nation came to Capt. C. leading an elegant white horse, with much ceremony he presented that horse to Capt. C. Capt. C. accepted it with pleasure, Yellept then indicated that he thought a Kittle would be satisfactory present in return.

Capt. C. explained that he could not, that we had but few Kittles and all were needed.

Yellept then admired Capt. C.'s sword, this cut Capt. C. to the bone, that sword is precious to him, he has worn it clear across the Continent, he has killed snakes with it and threatened Indians, it is near as much part of him as his arm.

Capt. C. was much distressed, Capt. Lewis said, Well, my friend, we knew we would come to this point, we have to start trading our equipment for our needs.

A little before sun set the Yakima Nation came in, 100 men and a few women, they joined the Walla Wallas in a circle and a feast of fish and roots.

Cruzzate brought out the fiddle, York danced first, Cruzzate was playing merry tunes and York slapped his feet and his thighs, he jumped and tumbled, his feet were fair flying, his white teeth glittered in the firelight.

York called us out for Virginy Reel, we did it proper, with bowing and scrapping and hands held high and skipping between the rows of dances, it was grand.

We then requested the Indians to dance, which they very cheerfully complied with, the whole assemblage of Indians, about 350 men, women, and children, sung and danced at the same time. The most of them stood in one place jumping up and down to the time of their music. Young warriors would leap into the middle of the circle and dance in a wild manner.

The Indians called for York again, he went to the circle and danced as the warriors did. Soon we were all joined in the circle swaying to their music. Capt. C. held Pomp in his arms as he danced.

This was a grand party, I am glad we stayed on.

April 30, '06.

Tonight we camped by a Stream in a copse of trees, we have the pleasure once more to find an abundance of good dry wood for the purpose of making a real fire. Drewyer killed an otter and a beaver in the stream.

Capt. C. was so pleased with his Beaver tail roasted and the comfortable fire he called for Pomp, Sacajawea brought him over and Capt. C. took him in his arms and sang a lullaby. Pomp was delighted, he was all smiles and laughs, Capt. C. handed him to York, saying, Here sing him one of your darky songs.

York sang a beautiful song in his deep voice, it was sad and full of sorrow, it ended on a note of finding a better life hereafter. Pomp wanted more, he pulled on York's ears, York gave him a spirited song, it rang through our Camp and out across the prairie. We all clapped.

Drewyer asked for Pomp, he held him and rocked him and sang a French song. Drewyer has a soft voice, in the middle of his song little Pomp's head fell back into his arms, he was asleep. Sacajawea took him off to bed.

I think of my child, it is maddening not knowing if my Baby is a boy or a girl, it is worse not knowing if he or she is alive and healthy. Drewyer tells me not to worry about those things I cannot effect, of course this is the best advice, except that it is impossible to carry out.

May 5, '06.

We traveled 20 miles today, we made Camp at the mouth of a stream which the Capts. name Colter Creek in honor of my friend John Colter, who hunted up this creek last fall and thus was the first white man to be on these waters.

Here there was two Indian lodges, one was much the

largest we have yet seen. It is 150 feet long and 15 feet wide, built of mats and straw, in the form of the roof of a house, it is closed at the ends but has small doors on the sides, the interior is one huge room without divisions. This lodge contained 30 Nez Perce families, their fires are kindled in a row in the center of the Lodge.

An old man came forward to harangue these People, he said Capt. C. had cured him of his pains in his legs last Fall and he extolled the virtues and skill of Capt. C. A number of them said that they had enjoyed great benefit from Capt. C.'s eye wash last Fall, the People began to gather round Capt. C. and apply to be his patient.

Well, my friend, Capt. Lewis said, it appears you are now their favorite physician. Capt. C. protested that the Indians had an exalted opinion of his doctoring, Capt. Lewis replied that considering our situation it appears to him that it is pardonable to continue this deception.

Capt. C. then announced that he would treat all the sick, but after they produced some dogs and other provisions in payment.

We were soon feasting on dog, tearing the meat from the bones by hand and stuffing it down so fast as possible. The Indians observed us with amazement. One fellow very impatiently threw a poor half-starved puppy nearly into Capt. Lewis's plate, he laughed very heartily at thus making fun of our eating Dog.

Capt. Lewis fair exploded, I have never seen him so Angry, he frightened me to see him so. He threw that puppy back in the Indian's face with great violence, then leaped on the fellow and beat him in the face and chest until the Indian cried out for Mercy. Capt. Lewis let him go, but seized his tomahawk and informed the fellow that he would kill him were he to repeat his insolence.

Capt. Lewis then set down, picked up his plate, and resumed eating his dog.

Capt. C. was sitting beside me, he was eating a scoop of roots only, he remains the single member of the Party who will not eat Dog, he commenced to laugh. Soon we were all laughing, even Capt. Lewis. The Indians were much astonished by all this.

After supper Capt. C. opened his pharmacy and treated his patients.

WAITING FOR THE SNOW TO MELT

May 8, '06.

This morning at breakfast Capt. C. was holding Pomp's hand, the boy let go and commenced to walk on his own, this was the first time, it delighted Capt. C. Pomp is growing fast, it is entrancing to watch him proceed from one Stage to the Next. He has begun to talk, his words are his own, the only one we can make out is "No Chinook." He says it with a fierce scowl on his face, this sends us into laughter which delights him to no end, he crawls or waddles from man to man growling, No Chinook.

Chief Twisted Hair and six of his warriors rode up, this is the Chief to whom we confided the care of our horses last fall. He had scarcely arrived when another Chief rode up, this was the Cut Nose with a party of his warriors.

The two Chiefs commenced to quarrel, they spoke in loud voices and an angry manner to one another for near an hour. We could make nothing of it, we proceeded on.

May 9, '06.

At dusk Twisted Hair's young men came in with 21 horses, the greater part were in fine order. The Capts. were delighted, we now have near 50 horses which is sufficient for our crossing of the mountains.

May 10, '06.

We proceeded to the lodge of the Broken Arm, we smoked with him. That Chief produced a present of two bushels of the quawmash roots dried, Capt. C. thanked him for this present, but informed him that we are not accustomed to living on roots alone and would become sick without meat. He therefore proposed exchanging one of our horses, which was in low order, for a young unbroken colt in tolerable order with a view to kill that colt for meat.

Then Broken Arm expressed himself as revolted at the idea of an exchange, he said he had many horses and if we wished to eat horses he should provide so many as we wished.

These People are indeed rich in horses, each warrior has so many as 50. When a man dies and is put on the scaffold, it is their custom to sacrifice all his Horses and place them around the scaffold. It is remarkable that except in the last extremity these People will not eat horse meat, the cause is their affection for their horses.

Broken Arm produced two fine fat young colts for us, we killed one and ate it, saving the other. Capt. Lewis declared that this is a much greater act of hospitality than we have witnessed from any nation since we have passed the Rocky Mountains, in short he said, it should be said to the immortal honor of the Nez Perce that they outshine all Indians in their hospitality.

May 12, '06.

We held shooting contests with the Indians this afternoon, none of us, save Drewyer, can match them even close in shooting the arrow, none of them can stay close to us in shooting a rifle. I hit the mark twice at 200 yards, only Drewyer did better. Colter says he can recall when I could not hit the Barn door from inside.

May 13, '06.

The Eagle and some of his friends challenged us to horse races today. They are excellent riders, only Shields could stay near them, a part of the race was down a steep bank to the river, Eagle descends at full speed which none of our Party dares attempt, I got thrown, I bruised my Hip.

Eagle is trying to teach me to shoot the arrow, he uses a hoop of willow bark as a target, it is the size of a small Dog, he hits it square at 100 yards, whilst it rolls across the prairie, I fail to hit it when it stands still at 50 yards.

Next we tried our strength at shooting arrows for distance, these Indians are able to send their arrows 400 yards, York is the only one amongst us who can come close to that.

I am teaching Eagle to shoot a rifle, he learns but slowly.

May 19, '06.

Many Indians come in today, we amuse ourselves with running the horses, the Eagle won the races. Capt. Lewis observed that some of these Nez Perce horses would be the equal to the finest blooded stock in Virginy.

May 26, '06.

Broken Arm came today for a visit, when he witnessed our distress he informed Capt. Lewis that the most of the horses running at large in this neighborhood belonged to himself, and whenever we were in want of meat we should kill any of them we wished. Capt. Lewis pronounced this a place of liberality which would do honor to a civilized man, indeed he said he thought there were many of our countrymen who would see us starve before making a similar act of liberality.

We dined on fresh horse meat tonight, it was much appreciated.

June 2, '06.

Our Merchandise is exhausted, this is a serious embarrassment as we do not have sufficient store of dried roots to sustain us in our passage where we were so hungry and cold last September.

The Capts. sent our best traders to the Nez Perce, these are McNeal and York, they are to obtain more roots. For that purpose the Capts. cut the buttons off their uniform coats, the Nez Perce prize those buttons.

Capt. C. does not mind much, but Capt. Lewis takes a great pride in his appearance, it near made him cry to cut off those buttons. We are reduced to beggarliness.

June 8, '06.

We have had races and etc. each day, this is by the Capts.' orders, they charge that those men who are not hunters have been getting rather lazy and slothful and need the exercise to prepare for the mountains. Sgt. Ordway says this is the way of the army officer, that they cannot bear it when they see a man idle.

We run short races and long. In the short ones Rubin Fields wins, he is the fastest among us, the Eagle near catches him sometimes. The long races are for one mile distance, in this Colter prevails among white men, but even Colter must give way to Little Hawk, who can run at his top speed for a mile or more.

June 9, '06.

The Capts. announced that we shall begin our voyage in the morning. Eagle and Little Hawk refused to be our guides, despite that we begged them, we offered them a rifle, they still would not consent. It is too early they say, there will not be sufficient grass for the horses.

June 11, '06.

We have come to the place the party enters the high mountains, we are encamped at a quawmash flat, the Capts. have decided to remain here for two or three days to allow the snow to melt and to stock up on meat.

June 13, '06.

Capt. C. completed today a census of the Indian Nations residing to the west of the Rocky Mountains, he estimates 80,000 souls.

Capt. C. says it shall be a long time before there are so many white settlers in this country, Capt. Lewis doubts that there will ever be so many whites here, he believes this shall always be an Indian country.

June 14, '06.

We are eager to go, but still apprehensive that the Snow and want of grass will prove a serious embarrassment to us, at least four days of our voyage through these mountains lies over heights and along a ledge of mountains never entirely destitute of snow. I recall Eagle's parting signs, which was that we should not make it, but Capt. Lewis declares that if it is in the compass of human power we shall.

OVER THE MOUNTAINS

June 16, '06.

We set off at 6 o'clock, in five hours we proceeded but seven miles up the mountain, fallen timber detained us much. We nooned it at a handsome little Glade on a small branch of Hungry Creek where there was some grass for our horses to graze.

After a hasty meal of roots we set out, the snow as we ascended became much deeper, it covered the trail. Fortunately, this snow was sufficiently firm to bear our horses, it is 8 feet deep.

Just before dark we arrived at this place, which is

where Capt. C. had killed and left the flesh of a horse for us last September. In this small glade there was little grass.

We made but 15 miles today. All exhausted.

June 17, '06.

This morning we ascended 3 miles when we found ourselves enveloped in snow from 12 to 15 feet deep, we were in winter with all its rigors.

Drewyer confesses he is confused, the Snow covers the trail completely, he is entirely doubtful of finding our path. Were we to become lost and wander in these mountains we should surely perish, in these circumstances the Capts. declared it madness to proceed without a guide.

June 18, '06.

We nooned it at the glade, after we ate the Capts. told me and Drewyer to proceed on ahead to the Nez Perce village so fast we could unencumbered by Pack horses, and there attempt to persuade Eagle and Little Hawk to become our guides. I doubted much that they would consent, Capt. C. instructed us that should they still refuse to guide us for the price of one rifle, to offer the reward of two other guns, and ten horses when we reached Traveler's Rest.

June 21, '06.

Eagle and Little Hawk come in today at noon, we attempted to persuade them to be our guides, they could not be induced.

June 22, '06.

Drewyer spent most of the day making signs with Eagle and Little Hawk, he informed them that the route was passable, that our difficulty was in not being able to follow the road, that if they would guide us we should make it.

They were not convinced, Drewyer then offered them two more guns and ten horses, this was more temptation than Eagle could stand, he should love to have a rifle of his own, he said he would do it. Little Hawk thereupon agreed to join.

I am delighted, first because we are getting started

again, next because these Indian boys are delightful companions.

June 24, '06.
We returned to the glade on Hungry Creek, we will begin our assault on the mountains in the morning.

June 25, '06.
Little Hawk was unwell this morning, Eagle told us to go ahead, that he and his brother would catch us up later. Capt. Lewis reluctantly gave the order to proceed on, he observed that such complaints with an Indian is generally the prelude to his abandoning the enterprise. I assured him that such was not the case in this instance.

We nooned it at a meadow on a branch of Hungry Creek after covering six miles of deep snow, while we dined Eagle and Little Hawk joined us, Capt. Lewis was pleased.

This afternoon, in consequence of the softness of the snow, we proceeded but five miles, we failed to reach our scaffolds on Hungry Creek.

🖋

June 26, '06.

The Eagle woke us before first light, he urged on us the need to press on, that we must now make forced marches if we were to reach Traveler's Rest before our horses expired and our roots give out. He indicated he had made this Passage every summer of his life, that it could not be made in less than seven days and that there were but one or two Places only where we should discover grass.

Later in the evening, much to our satisfaction and to the comfort of our poor horses, we arrived at the desired spot, which is on the steep side of a mountain next to a good spring, this mountain has a south-facing aspect, here the snow was melted, the grass young and tender, the horses could scarcely wait for us to unload their baggage so eager were they to graze.

From this exposed side we can see vast distances to the east, south, and west, the whole expanse exposes naught but more mountains to be seen, all glistening in the sunset, this is a view without parallel, it is beautiful in the extreme, but I could not enjoy it sufficiently, I was too tired.

June 27, '06.

We mounted our horses and proceeded on. Eagle is the most admirable pilot, wherever the snow has disappeared the road appears, he never loses it. Twice I fell asleep on my horse, I fell off into snow banks.

June 28, '06.

We were off early as usual, at 13 miles we came to a mountain with an untimbered side facing South, here we found an abundance of grass for our horses. All being much fatigued and Eagle informing that there was no grass within reach of our travel in the after part of the day, the Capts. determined to remain here to allow the horses to graze and the men to rest.

I took a nap, this is the first nap I have had since I was on this Expedition, it was welcome. I woke hungry as a bear in the Spring, there were only roots to eat.

June 29, '06.

This morning we pursued the heights of the ridge, it terminated at the distance of 5 miles, we descended the mountain to the waters of the Kooskooskee River, when we descended from the ridge we bid adieu to the snow. The Nez Perce have a weir on this place, but there were no fish, we nooned it on roots.

In the afternoon we ascended a very steep acclivity of a mountain 2 miles, we came to the quawmash flats and halted to graze our horses and dine, having traveled 12 miles. This is a handsome little plain of about 50 acres, plentifully stocked with quawmash, Sacajawea gathered in some roots. A beautiful stream winds through it, the grass is good.

We continued our march seven miles down the mountain, we proceeded only with difficulty due to the fallen timber, still we were all in high spirits to know that the end was in view.

At seven miles we came to the warm springs, a sight as our first glimpse of the great Pacific Ocean. This is a handsome little quawmash plain of 10 acres, surrounded by huge boulders, Traveler's Rest Creek flows through it, here there are hot springs near the bank of the creek. The Nez Perce have made a bath at this place by placing rocks to stop the run, the springs are hot.

Immediately upon our arrival Eagle and Little Hawk

tore off their shirts and leggings and plunged into the bath, it was near too hot to touch, but they remained in for near 30 minutes. Drewyer remarked that he had never seen a happier Indian in his life, he thought he might try a soak for himself, soon he was lying back with just his nose and eyes above the water, his look was one of the purest contentment.

Charbono allowed as how his old bones could use a soak, he joined the party of bathers. Colter was next, then both Capts. joined.

Next we were astonished to see Eagle and Little Hawk leap out of the pool and dash across to the creek where they plunged into the water as cold as ice. They let out whoops and Hollers and Cries of Joy, they splashed one another, they were crazy. After a few minutes of foolery, they ran back to the hot pool and plunged back into it heaving great sighs of relief.

Soon, the whole party, even the Capts. were running back and forth from the ice cold water to the near boiling hot pool, I joined in the game, it was refreshing to a remarkable degree, an hour before I thought I would join just as soon as die as take one more step, now I am prepared to join Colter, who says he is ready to go back over the mountains if the Capts. so direct, he feels that good.

June 30, '06.

We made a leisurely march down the creek in the after part of the day, we came to Traveler's Rest, here we shall rest for two days. The Capts. presented our guides with the guns promised to them, they were as happy as we.

RETURN TO THE MANDANS

July 1, '06.

The game is plenty, by noon we had 12 deer, Capt. C. declares that this is like returning to the land of the living.

The Capts. announce that from this place the Party shall divide, nine men will accompany Capt. Lewis on an Exploration of Maria's River with a view to discover how far north that River extends. The remainder of the Party will accompany Capt. C. on an Exploration of the Yellowstone River. The two Parties will meet at the junction of the Missouri and Yellowstone Rivers.

Capt. Lewis's route is the more dangerous, as it will

carry him into the country of the Blackfeet, when he asked for volunteers all the Party stepped forward. He choose Drewyer to be his principle hunter, Capt. C. thereupon declared that I would accompany him as Principle Hunter for his Party.

This is the first time I shall be separated from Capt. Lewis since July of 1803, it gives me great anxiety even though I have the utmost faith in Capt. C. I shall miss Drewyer near as much, it is a weight of responsibility to be the principle hunter without his Guidance.

July 6, '06.

Today we arrived at the dividing ridge that separates Clark's River from the creeks that flow into the Jefferson and thence to Three Forks and the Missouri. Sacajawea informs that our new route is a shorter one to our caches on Jefferson River.

Capt. C. observed that the route Sacajawea advised can't possibly be much worse than the one we used, he was convinced she was right when we discovered ourselves on an old buffalo road with the skulls scattered on it, for the Buffalo always follow the best route.

July 8, '06.

Sacajawea has proved to be so dependable a guide as Eagle and Little Hawk, at noon today we came to our cache on the river.

For the last two miles Colter and the smokers were running their Horses, when we arrived at the caches they scarcely took the time to take their saddles off those horses before they were off at a mad dash for the caches, they started digging furiously, in short order they had uncovered the baggage, they tore off the skins to get at the tobacco, in an instant all had their pipes full and were puffing so hard as could be done.

I never saw a man so Happy as John Colter, he sat with his back to a tree, the smile on his face as one of the purest Contentment. So it was with all the users of the weed, they put up so much smoke Capt. C. remarked that the Indians would think this was a War Party.

Tonight at the fire Colter was puffing away, he said, George, Don't you want to try some?

I was sore tempted, anything that gives so many men

so much pleasure must be good, I thought. I agreed to try a pipe.

As Sgt. Pryor suggested I went easy at first, taking in only a small bit of smoke, still it sent me into a coughing fit, it was vile. But when I managed to get some down it sent my head spinning, I could feel it clear down to my toes, it was most enjoyable.

July 23, '06.

At noon we arrived at the Three Forks, one hour later Capt. C. and the canoe Party came up.

From this place, Capt. C. announced, ten men under the direction of Sgt. Ordway shall set out in the canoes for the Great Falls. There they shall uncover the caches, make the portage, and meet with Capt. Lewis and his Party at the mouth of the Maria's River.

The balance of the Party with 49 horses and a colt will go overland to the point where we cut the Yellowstone River, where we shall make canoes for the voyage to the meeting of the Yellowstone and the Missouri, at which place we shall join with Capt. Lewis and his contingent.

July 15, '06.

We pursued the old buffalo road, it took us over a low dividing ridge to the head of a water course which runs into the Yellowstone, at 2 o'clock today we arrived at the Yellowstone. This river runs out of a big rugged mountain to the South all covered with Snow, Capt. C. regrets we have not the time to spare to examine up this river to its source, he remarks that Colter, who is so determined to return to this country, can explore it next year.

July 26, '06.

Windsor, who was our sentinel from 2 o'clock in the morning, fell asleep. When we awoke we discovered the Crows had driven off all our horses.

God damn it, said Sgt. Pryor.

Windsor said he was sorry.

That does us no good, replied Sgt. Pryor.

Sgt. Pryor said we must get after them immediately if we were to catch them. Windsor protested that this was a War Party, that three men were not enough to challenge those Crows.

We have guns, I said, and it is near certain that they do

not, even if they do they can't shoot straight, Let's get going.

We pursued those tracks five miles, the Indians there divided into two parties. We continued in pursuit of the largest party five miles further, we were pressing so fast as our legs could bear it, we were out of breath and panting. Finally, Sgt. Pryor admitted that their was not the smallest chance of overtaking the thieves.

We returned to the river which we struck at a handsome bottom, at this place there is a remarkable rock, it is 200 feet high and 400 paces in circumference, from its top I had a most extensive view in every direction, were I to attempt to describe the numbers of animals I saw I should not be believed.

On this rock we found Capt. C. had carved his name and the date, July 25, 1806, this means he passed yesterday, this was a disappointment in the extreme as we had hoped to meet with him and proceed on with the canoe party. Now we shall not catch him up, he is ahead and undoubtedly making rapid progress in his canoes.

We made our camp and took stock of our situation, which is Serious. We have no axes, we cannot make canoes. We have only our knives, guns, balls and powder and knapsacks. It is near 1,000 miles to the Mandan Village.

Windsor was downcast, he thought we were goners for certain, the Crow will get us sure.

Sgt. Pryor said, No, we are experienced travelers, we have plenty of game, we have but to follow the river and we shall make it to the Mandans.

And, he added, we are not without resources, consider all those buffalo that are all around us.

What do you propose, asked Windsor, that we should ride buffalo to the Mandans?

Sgt. Pryor laughed, Yes, he said, in a way. We will make bull boats like the Mandan do and ride them down the river.

I thought that a good idea, Windsor was doubtful, but Pryor and I are determined to try, we shall get at it in the morning.

July 28, '06.
Yesterday I killed a bull, we have made our boat in the form and shape of the Mandan boats, 2 sticks tied

together so as to form a round hoop large enough for the Skin to cover. We made two of those hoops one for the top and the other for the bottom, we then crossed Sticks of the same size at right angles and fastened them with a thong to each hoop and also where each Stick crosses the other. Next we took the green skin and drew it tight over the frame and fastened it with thongs to the brims so as to form a perfect basin.

The boat is capable of carrying 8 men and their loads.

Sgt. Pryor decided to make a second boat in the event we meet with some accident in passing down the Yellowstone, which may have rapids on it. I killed another buffalo and we made a second boat, we shall carry one of the rifles and some of the ammunition in it so as to never be without even should we tip in our boat.

July 30, '06.

We set out this morning, our boats answer perfectly, they float like corks, they take on not a single drop of water even in the Shoals which are numerous but not bad. Waves raised from the hardest winds do not affect them, though they are difficult to steer, much more so than a canoe.

Aug. 1, '06.

A most pleasant day. Out on the river we escape the musketeers, we bob along quite gaily, indeed today we were singing, when it gets too Hot we splash cold water on our heads, we have long talks about what to eat, whether Elk or deer or buffalo.

Aug. 6, '06.

At noon today we had to pole to shore to wait for a gangue of buffalo to pass the river, the river is near a half mile wide, notwithstanding this width the buffalo were stretched from one shore to the other as thick as they could swim, it took near an hour for this immense herd to cross.

This after we came to the meeting of the Yellowstone and Missouri Rivers, the remains of Capt. C.'s camp indicate that he is not far ahead.

Aug. 8, '06.

Sgt. Pryor had us up before the dawn, we set out in the dark, Sgt. Pryor thinks Capt. C. must be close by.

At 8 o'clock we saw a joyous sight, there were the canoes pulled on shore, the Party was cooking breakfast at their camp. We were overjoyed, Capt. C. greeted us with surprise, Sgt. Pryor reported the theft of our horses. Capt. C. wished it had not been but he was soon reconciled to our fate, he said he was glad of our ingenuity and that we had made it Safe.

Capt. C. and Party had been here some days past, they are waiting on Capt. Lewis who has not yet joined, Capt. C. is worried for his friend.

Colter gave me a big hug, he was glad to see me, he gives me some tobacco, we have been without for five days, I find I missed it much.

I recollected that in our haste to be off this morning I had left my knapsack behind, it contained the journal, Capt. C. gave me permission to go back to retrieve it. I am glad to have it, I should be distressed in the extreme to lose it after spending so much effort on it.

❧

Aug. 11, '06.

At noon today two white men in a canoe come up, they were Joseph Dixon and F. Hancock from the Illinois, they are trappers who started up the Missouri in the summer of 1804. They escaped and spent the next year with the Mandans.

They had no news of the U. States, they did have unwelcome news from the Indian Nations, the Mandans and the Minnitarees were at war with the Ricaras.

I asked them did they meet Peme, did she have a child, what was it a boy or a girl, the words gushed out.

Yes, Dixon said, he had noticed a young squaw in the lodge of the Mandan Chief who had a child, he had not heard her name nor could he say with confidence whether the baby was a boy or a girl. But Hancock added there were lots of squaws in the Mandan village that had half-breed children that was born in the Fall of 1805, that so far as he could see the Corps of Discovery had become the fathers of a whole new Generation of Mandans.

This set near every man of the Party to inquiring about their favorite squaws, the men from Illinois pleaded that they could not tell one squaw from the other, they could not answer the questions.

York wanted to know was there any black babies. Many, replied Dixon. York was some set up.

For my part I am satisfied that Peme is alive and well, our Baby too, this is wonderful news. It makes me sick with desire to get to the Mandans as soon as possible, where oh where is Capt. Lewis?

Colter has persuaded these men to return to the Mandans with us, there he says they can replenish their supplies, then they can set out again for the Yellowstone Country to winter over and trap and hunt and Explore. Colter will join them.

George, you come too, Colter says, we shall make it a merry party, he waved his arm to indicate the scene around us which is indeed beautiful. Think of the fun we can have in this Paradise, Colter says.

And the money we can make, added Dixon, this is the primmest Beaver country there ever was.

Yes, I said. Yes, I will join you. I have decided that the wilderness is my true home.

The words just came out, I had not thought about

them. Now I feel the greatest relief, I have made my decision on a question that has plagued me for months past, I now know what I shall do and where I belong.

Aug. 12, '06.

This morning I informed Capt. C. that my intention was to turn back with Colter once we got to the Mandans.

Inadmissible, he declared.

I protested that he had agreed to allow Colter to turn back, why not me?

We shall need every man to get past the Sioux, he replied, we cannot afford to allow any to turn back.

Why does Colter get to, I demanded to know.

Because, Capt. C. said, Colter has been determined to turn back for more than a year now, Capt. Lewis and I have long since agreed that he can do so.

This is unfair, I exclaimed.

So is life, he replied. He said he would not hear another word on the Subject.

At noon today Capt. Lewis and Party came into sight, there was much rejoicing and gaiety to see them, we were dancing and shouting and firing off our pieces on the river bank, when the canoes pulled to we were alarmed to see Capt. Lewis was lying on his stomach, he could not move.

Drewyer and York carried him to camp, we all gathered round in great concern. Capt. Lewis said not to worry, that his wound was painful but not serious. It appears that Cruzzate, who is near-sighted, and has the use of but one eye, mistook the Capt., who was wearing an elk skin shirt, for an Elk, and Cruzzate shot Capt. Lewis in the buttocks.

Capt. C. dressed the wounds, he said it was clean, that the ball in passing through hit no bone, he thought recovery should be slow but complete.

With this welcome information we all sat down to hear the story of Capt. Lewis's adventure.

The sum of it is that it was a disaster. Maria's River turns straight to the West and enters the mountains far short of fifty degrees. Capt. Lewis shall have to inform the President that Louisiana does not extend to the Saskacawan country.

Capt. Lewis named his camp at the northernmost point of the Maria's River, Camp Disappointment.

He left that place on July 26, that evening while crossing the plains he encountered a Party of 8 Blackfeet warriors. They appeared friendly, Capt. Lewis camped with them and smoked.

In the morning the Blackfeet attempted to rob his Party, they had a fight, and an Indian ran off with Rubin's gun, Rubin gave chase and caught up to that man and killed him with his knife. Capt. Lewis in the meanwhile gave chase to two Indians running off his horses, he shot and killed one of those Indians. The remainder of the Blackfeet did run off with the horses but Drewyer managed to retain the horses of the Indians, the Party mounted those horses and rode 120 miles in 24 hours to get to the mouth of the Maria's, expecting all the while the whole tribe of Blackfeet at any moment.

Tonight I asked Rubin what it was like to kill a man. He said it wasn't any different than plunging a knife into a deer or Elk.

I said I couldn't believe that.

He said, All right, I will confess. When I saw that bastard running off with my gun, my only source of food and protection in this Wilderness and my horse, Why, George, at that moment I wanted to kill him before he killed me, and it wasn't like hunting at all, except if it were the grizzlies.

He stopped. He said, after a bit, that it had all the excitement of hunting the grizzly bear.

Except, I said, that he was running away from you.

With everything that stood between me and a slow horrible death on that prairie, Rubin replied.

What happened then, I asked.

Rubin said he ran after the thief, that he never ran so fast, that when he caught up he plunged his knife into the heart of that warrior, and that the blood came pumping out in great spurts.

It was the greatest moment of all, Rubin said, better even than seeing the Pacific Ocean, or getting across the Rocky Mountains. He laughed and pulled out of his sack a dirty, bloody scalp, he tossed it at me. Here is the bastard himself, he said.

I could not believe it, I blurted out. You Didn't!

Damn right I did, he replied. I told you my blood was up.

I don't think I could do that, I said.

Course you can, George, Rubin laughed. You stay in this wilderness with Colter and you sure as hell will be lifting scalps.

I don't believe it, I said. I don't believe you have to sink to the level of the savage to live in the Wilderness.

Aug. 14, '06.

We proceeded on to the Mandan Village, we came to on a sand bar opposite the Mandans. So soon as we landed the Mandans began to cross in their bull boats, there was waving and crying and shouting, the men all waded out to help bring in the boats.

I saw Peme, I swam out to her boat, she looked down at me and laughed, my heart near stopped she was so beautiful, her hair flung in cues on each side down to her waist, her face was aglow, painted with vermillion, her dark eyes so big as a fawn's, her teeth white as snow, her dress was a beaded doe skin with fringes, this was a vision.

She had on her cradleboard, she turned and there was my child! I could see but the fact, I reached up and set my hand into the cradleboard, I felt between the legs, I have a Son!

We pulled the bull boat ashore, the men were setting off up and down the river bank with squaws, the most of them had cradleboards. Peme and me climbed the bank and went out on the prairie. At first we were shy, she set down the cradleboard. Soon we started talking, she trying English, me in Shoshone, she said our son was born in October, he is near a year old already. I lay down, he crawled over my chest and pulled my beard, he is a good strong lad, he has a handsome look.

Does he have a name, I asked.

No, she replied, she has been waiting for me to give a name.

Robinson, I said, it is Robinson.

Peme could not say it, she thought I meant Robin, that he was named for the bird.

Robin it shall be, I declared, that covers two of my heroes, Robinson Crusoe and Robin Hood. I tried to explain who they were but had to give it up. So far as she is concerned, our son is named for the bird. This makes her happy, as she says the Robin is full of bounce and joy.

Peme put Robin back in his cradleboard and turned to me and smiled and opened her Arms and my heart beat, my member swelled and jerked, I roared like one of those old buffalo bulls in running season, oh the happiness!

We returned to the camp, Capt. C. had sent Charbono to the Minnitaree village to request the Chiefs to come in for a council.

In the after part of the day the Chiefs came in, they brought presents of corn. Capt. C. then spoke to them, he requested that some of them should come to visit their Great Father in Washington City and receive gifts.

All the Chiefs declined, they were afraid of the Sioux below, who would kill them.

Capt. C. harangued them, they would not agree to go. Finally, Little Crow, a chief, said he would go, that he believed Capt. C. when he said the white men would protect him from the Sioux and provide a War Party to be certain of his return next summer. He said he would be ready to go in the morning.

Colter meanwhile had acquired a supply of tobacco, it was time for him to set off back up the river. All gathered around Colter to wish him every success. He has picked out his squaw, he says she was the mother of his child, who is a boy which he had named Merry Weather.

The Capts. give him some powder and lead, every man tried to find something to give him, we have nothing to Give, Drewyer gave him a whet stone, Rubin Fields gave him some thread, others give buttons & etc.

I give him Mr. Boone's knife. I told him she was a good one, to take care of her, that I would want her back next summer when he brings in his Furs and I come up from St. Louis with Little Crow. He promised he would see me a year from today.

Colter and the Illinois men loaded in their balls and powder, corn and tobacco.

Colter was looking west, he never looked back.

Peme asked tonight, her face was turned down, she spoke so low I could scarcely hear her, she wondered, would I stay?

I said No, she commenced to cry. I told her that I would be back soon and explained the plan, she lifted her face, she had tears but she was smiling. A year goes by quick, she said.

We are all with our squaws, there have been shouts and groans up and down the river all night long. The sun is near up, my son and Peme sleep beside me, the river rolls on, all is contentment.

Aug. 16, '06.

We walked to the village of Little Crow, to Capt. C.'s astonishment Little Crow said he had declined going down river.

The Capts. were much put out. Peme wished to know what was the matter, I explained to her, she said she could provide a chief for the Capts., she said she could persuade Mandan Chief to come down.

I reported this to the Capts., they said she should try, we set out immediately. At Mandan Chief's village, Peme led me into the Chief's lodge, he greeted her warmly, he listened to her invitation, he said he would go if I promised to help him return and if he could bring his wife and son and Peme and Robin.

We ran back to our camp. I told the Capts. They agreed at once.

My cup runneth over, as my Father would say. I shall

take Peme and Robin to Washington City, we can pay a call on my parents, we can see civilization and then return to Missouri, my joy is boundless, my body shakes with it.

Aug. 17, '06.

This morning we dropped down to Mandan Chief's village, 1/2 mile on the south side, we walked to the lodge of the Chief, he was surrounded by his friends. The men were sitting in a circle smoking and the women crying. Mandan Chief sent his baggage with his wife and son, we all went down to the canoes. Capt. C. has lashed two canoes together by poles so as to make them steady for the Chief and his family and mine.

The parting of Sacajawea and Peme was truly moving, they embraced and cried. Sacajawea through her tears had me promise to look after Peme, to take care of her, & etc. Charbono advised me to remember always that Peme was a squaw, to treat her as such and not to spoil her.

We made 18 miles today, we are on our way home. I

have a wife and child to introduce to my Parents, Capt. Lewis says I shall meet the President when Mandan Chief meets him, I will be returning next summer to the Wilderness, I will sleep with Peme in my arms tonight, Robin beside us, and a smile on my face.

THE HOME STRETCH

Aug. 20, '06.

We proceeded on very well today, we made 81 miles.

Peme is in good spirits, she turns to smile at me or point out game, bluffs, & etc., she claps her hands in delight at new sights. Mandan Chief is more composed, he grunts from time to time.

For myself, my happiness is Total.

Aug. 21, '06.

At noon today we hove into site of the Ricara Village, we pulled to shore where we were saluted by the Ricara

Chiefs, also by Cheyenne Chiefs who were encamped on the bluffs back from the river.

Capt. C. informed the Ricaras and Cheyennes where we had been and what we had done.

Then he told the Ricaras that he was very sorry to hear that they were not on friendly terms with their neighbors, the Mandans, and had not listened to what we had said to them, but had Suffered their young men to join the Sioux, who had killed 8 Mandans and stolen horses. He asked how could they expect other nations would be at peace with them when they themselves would not listen to what their Great Father had told them.

Mandan Chief made a harangue, he explained the cause of the Misunderstanding between his Nation and the Ricaras, informing them of his wish to be on the most friendly terms. The Cheyenne Chief spoke next, he accused both nations of being in fault. Capt. C. replied that if the Cheyennes wished to be happy that they must Shake off all intimacy with the Sioux and attend to what we had told them. This they promised to do.

We returned to the River, at this place the One Arm, a Ricara Chief, spoke to Mandan Chief in a loud, threatening tone. Capt. C., whose blood was up, informed the Ricaras that the Mandans had opened their ears to and followed our councils, that this Chief, the Mandan Chief, was on his way to see their Great Father, and was under our protection, that if any injury was done to him by any nation that we should kill them all.

Aug. 28, '06.

Capt. C. has made a list of the animals of which we have not either the skins or skeletons of, he has directed the hunters to obtain examples of Mule Deer, barking squirrels, antelope, and the Magpie.

Whilst the hunters were searching for specimens, Capt. C. permitted me to join Peme and Mandan Chief's squaw on an island, there we gathered in plums, we took more plums than the party could eat in two days, they are the most of them large and well flavored.

Aug. 30, '06.

At dawn we collected the specimens, the animals had come to the river to drink. We set out, we did not catch up to the Party until 6 o'clock.

Peme was in great agitation, she told me that this morning the Party had passed a band of Sioux warriors, near 80 or 90 of them, all armed with fuses and bows and arrows, they fired off their guns as a Salute, which Salute the Party returned.

Those Sioux wished the Party to come ashore, instead, Peme said, Capt. C. had the Party come to on the opposite bank. Three warriors swam over, they said their Chief was Black Buffalo, he was the worse of all the Sioux we encountered over two years.

Capt. C. told those Indians that they had been deaf to our councils and had ill treated us as we ascended the river two summers past, that they had abused all the whites who had visited them since, that they were bad People and he, Capt. C., should not allow them to cross to the Side on which the Party lay. He directed those Indians to swim back and inform Black Buffalo that if any of them come near our camp we should kill them certainly.

The Party continues on, at two miles seven Sioux were on the top of a hill and blackguarded the Party, those Sioux said the Party should come ashore and that they would kill all the men. Capt. C. instructed the Party to ignore the Sioux, no notice was taken of them.

Well, I said, we never even saw a Sioux and here I am, Peme was pleased. We played with Robin, and then with each other, all is contentment.

Sept. 4, '06.

At noon today we came to at Floyd's Bluff below the entrance of Floyd's River, we ascended the hill where we found that the grave had been opened by the natives and left half covered. All were indignant. We dug a deeper grave and placed Sgt. Floyd's remains Safe.

As we descended the hill Capt. Lewis observed that only one man had died, that this was perhaps his proudest boast.

A strong head wind, we made but 36 miles today.

Sept. 5, '06.

The mosquitoes being so excessively tormenting we were packed and off before daylight, and proceeded on very well. We made 73 miles today.

Capt. Lewis has suffered a setback, Capt. C. says he

extended himself too far in climbing Sgt. Floyd's Bluff yesterday.

Mandan Chief and his squaw are weary of this journey, they wish to turn back. I am sorry to record that Peme too is full of tears, she had not realized we should travel so far, she wished to return to the Mandan village where she can be with Sacajawea and can wait for my return next summer.

I attempt to explain to her that we cannot turn back, that it is inadmissible, she will not understand. The Capts. told Mandan Chief, as I told Peme, of all the presents they shall receive, that they shall meet the Great Father, and see the strange and wonderful sights, it made no impression. They wished to go home.

I talked with Peme for near two hours, it failed to have an effect, indeed she now wants me to return with her, we shall go on to meet with Colter, she says, and she can visit her people the Shoshones in the mountains. We could never get past the Sioux, I said, she said we did it once, we can do it again. The Sioux are out hunting, she said. That is why we did not encounter them on the River, only a hunting party. So it went until midnight when I gave up. She will have to come along, like it or not, so too Mandan Chief and his family.

Sept. 9, '06.

Peme continues to sulk and scold, she repeats her wish to go home, I no longer attempt to dissuade her, soon she will realize she must accept her Fate.

Sept. 12, '06.

At noon today we met a party going to the Ricaras, one of this party was Mr. Gravelines, the Ricaras' interpreter who had gone down with the Ricara Chief in the Spring of 1805 with Corp. Warfington on the keelboat. He had with him instructions to teach the Ricaras agriculture and to make every inquiry about the Corps of Discovery.

Mr. Gravelines, who was delighted to see us, had unwelcome news, it was that the Ricara Chief who had visited the U. States had unfortunately died at the City of Washington. This information will certainly have a bad effect on the Ricaras, Capt. C. wished much that it were not so.

Mandan Chief was much alarmed when he heard this news, he asked to be taken back to his village.

Inadmissible, Capt. C. proclaimed.

Peme and Mandan Chief's squaw commenced to cry, they did not wish to go to the City of Washington to die, I took Peme off to convince her to go on, I promised her that no harm could come to her, Had I not always been a man of my word, I asked.

She said she was still afraid, I told her she knew that the Ricara Chief was an old man, that his time had come, that he would have died just as dead in his own village, she admitted that such was the case.

I told her to tell that to Mandan Chief, which was done, the Chief then informed the Capts. that he was ready to go on. Capt. C. said I had done good work, Capt. Lewis said I should be a Diplomat, I replied that my only wish was to complete this voyage and return to the Wilderness.

Sept. 13, '06.

Mr. Gravelines gave us each a dram in the morning at breakfast, we set off at 8 o'clock in a very merry Condition.

The wind proving too high we came to after making only 18 miles. When we made camp I discovered that as a Consequence of taking the dram I had forgot my horn and pouch, my powder ball and knife, and my journal.

Capt. C. said I was the most forgetful man he ever met, he sent me back for the articles. Peme came with me, it took near five hours to get to the campsite of last night, when we arrived it was coming on dark, we recovered the articles, then we rested while Peme fed Robin. The moon shined on the river, it was a most pleasing aspect.

We started back, Peme never faltered, despite that she was carrying Robin, she never lets me carry him. I believe she can hike further than I can. We arrived at the camp past midnight, there being no point to attempting to sleep I write in my journal, which I shall never ever hereafter neglect to keep on my person.

Sept. 18, '06.

At 10 o'clock today we came to, Peme had seen poppaws on the bank, we gathered a considerable quantity. We have no meat but the Party to a man wished to avoid sending out hunters, we want to get on to the Settlements which are but 150 miles ahead. We have one biscuit per man only, we told the Capts. we can live very well on the poppaws, we do not wish to allow one minute even of daylight to pass without making progress. The Capts. say this pleases them much, we made 52 miles today.

Sept. 19, '06.

Peme is recovered her usual cheerfulness, Mandan Chief appears reconciled to his fate.

Sept. 20, '06.

At noon today, Shields, in the lead Canoe, let out a shout, soon we were all Shouting with our might, Shields had spotted cows on the banks. There was the greatest joy, we all got to talking about how good milk was going to taste.

Soon we came in sight of the little French village called La Charrette, we raised another Shout and Sprung to our oars, we landed. Sgt. Ordway requested that we be permitted to fire off our Guns, this was allowed, we discharged 3 rounds with a hearty cheer.

The citizens answered in kind, every person, both French and American seemed to express great pleasure at our return, they acknowledged themselves to be much astonished in seeing us return, they had supposed we were lost long since, and were entirely given out by every person.

Except one, Mr. Daniel Boone, who came to meet us and said he never had the slightest doubt we should return. He said he was so proud of us, he had made many inquiries which the Capts. answered so well as they could, he was entranced by their answers. He asked me, did his knife do good service, it did indeed, I replied. I told him it was now with my friend John Colter in the Wilderness, he was much pleased by this information.

He asked me did I see any beautiful sites, I said there were so many it should take me a week to describe. What was the most beautiful, he asked. The Pacific Ocean, I replied.

The Citizens provided us with a supper of Beef, flour and some pork, and milk, this made a very agreeable supper, this is our first beef since May of 1804, Drewyer pronounced it good but said it was not so good as buffalo. It beats spoiled Elk, said Rubin Fields.

As it was like to rain we accepted beds in the houses of the village, the most of the men discovered that they cannot sleep on a bed, they retired to the floor. Peme and Robin and me sleep under our skin stretched over poles, I tried a feather bed, I could not lie on it for a few moments only, this is a feature of civilization that is a great mistake.

I am beginning to wonder, can I live in Civilization?

Sept. 22, '06.

At 10 o'clock it ceased raining and we set out, we proceeded down to Fort Belle Fountane, which has been erected by Gen'l Wilkinson at this place there is a public store in which are kept many thousands of dollars' worth of Indian Goods, here the Capts. saw some of their old friends from the Army, we were very kindly received by these officers.

The barber gives us all haircuts, we scarcely recognize one another, Robin cried at the site of me. I feel naked without my beard and my hair cut from my shoulders.

The officers provide us with clothes and tailors, we all look like Indians according to them, one said we appeared to be 32 Robinson Crusoes.

Sept. 23, '06.

This morning Mandan Chief and his squaw, Peme and Robin and me, and the Capts. went to the public store to furnish the Indians with Clothes. The Mandan Chief chose for himself a tall top hat which has a great plume extending near two feet above, an artillery officer's great coat which has big epaulets on the shoulders and extends to his knees, it is bound at the waste with a red sash and has large brass buttons. For leggings he chose a pair of trousers with red stripe, they button in the front. Capt. Lewis had to explain to him the purpose of those Buttons.

Mandan Chief was much pleased with his appearance.

Peme chose for herself a dress which is of wool and dyed blue, she accepted a necklace of blue beads and scarlet pantaloons, when she was dressed she came to Robin who commenced to cry at the sight of her, when she took him to feed him he cried more. She declared that the fault was the wool, which scratches, she liked it no better than Robin, she removed the dress and resumed wearing her antelope skin dress.

For my part I think she looks much the finer in antelope than in wool.

As we past Camp Wood, Drewyer, who was beside me in the canoe remarked, Well George, I well recall when we were there, you were so green I thought you would never make a Hunter, now look you are perhaps the best Hunter I ever met.

Sgt. Ordway who was behind us said he thought I should never make a soldier, now I was a fine soldier, I had turned from the Baby of the Party into a man he would trust his life to.

Capt. C. said he supposed I had done all right.

Capt. Lewis said for his part he could recall the day I first approached him in Pittsburgh, he had thought it amusing in the extreme that I should think myself capable of being a part of the Corps of Discovery, he said he congratulated himself for being so wise to choose me.

I was too embarrassed to answer, I dug my paddle deeper, my heart was pounding fast, I was glad Peme has learned some English so that she can know what these men think of me.

We descended the Mississippi to St. Louis and arrived at this place at noon. We fired off our pieces as a Salute to the Town, when we came to at the landing we were met by all the residents who give us a hearty welcome. There is to be a dinner and ball for us.

We have completed our voyage of Discovery. We discover the best discovery of all, that we are all heroes.

DOWNCASTED

Jan'y 1, '08.

It has been 15 months since I wrote in this journal, I now feel a necessity to record the Events that have since transpired.

On the 10th of Oct. '06 we received our discharge from the Army, our pay, and our 320 acre plots in Missouri. Werner, Shields and some others set out immediately to take up their farms, the most of the others did as I did and sold their deeds. Sgt. Pryor discovered that his wife had died, he therefore sold his deed and enlisted again in the Army, he was promoted to Ensign. Some others also decided to remain as soldiers, these included Brattan, Sgt. Gass, Windsor, and Willard and myself.

My plan was to stick with the Army until we had been to Washington City and returned Mandan Chief to his People, at that time the Capts. said I could receive my Discharge and take Peme to join Colter in the Wilderness. Drewyer, Wiser, and Collins all intended to return to the Wilderness also, they would set out in the Spring of '07.

At the end of October of '06, our Party set out for the City of Washington. We consisted of the Capts., Sgt. Ordway, Labiche, Frasier and York, myself, the Mandan Chief and his squaw, Peme and Robin. We had packhorses to carry our specimens, seeds, and plants, maps, skins & etc., a good road to follow, villages and farms along the way, in short a splendid voyage.

We stopped in Louisville, where General George Rogers Clark greeted us, he put his arm around his brother and pronounced his complete satisfaction with all that had been done, he warned the Capts. to look Sharp in the City of Washington, he said that they should expect nothing but ill treatment and no gratitude from the Gov't. The Citizens of Louisville held a grand ball in our honor, it was pleasing but not so much so as the Ball in St. Louis as the Citizens requested Capt. Clark to not bring York, they made much of the Mandan Chief, but they were cruel to Peme when they discovered that she was my wife. We left the Ball.

Drewyer in short was right, it would be foolish of me to even contemplate living East of the Mississippi River with an Indian wife and son.

Capt. C. left the Party at this time, he went to Fincastle in Virginy, he informed that his intention was to court Miss Julia Hancock of that city after who he had named the Big Horn River.

The remainder of the Party traveled with Capt. Lewis to his home in Charlottesville, while we were there Capt. Lewis took us all to Mr. Jefferson's mansion at Monticello, there we were pleased to see the Mandan headdresses and clothes and buffalo skins and other specimens that had been sent back in the Spring of '05.

We celebrated the Christmas at Capt. Lewis's home in Locust Hill, we had turkey and ham and sweet potatoes, it was sumptuous. Peme received from Capt. Lewis's mother a dress of silk with ruffles & etc., she liked it much better than the wool dress, she looked fine. Capt. Lewis's mother gave Robin a toy wagon with a string, he pulled that wagon all day, Mrs. Lewis taught him to say "wagon," he repeated the word constantly, this was his first word.

I bought a necklace of pearls for Peme, Mrs. Lewis helped me select it. I bought a rifle for the Mandan Chief and a fine addition of Poor Richard's Almanac for Capt. Lewis. He gave me a copy of Mr. Wm. Byrd's Histories of the Dividing Line, he allowed as how he thought I should be surprised to discover much those men fought with each other, and that I should be pleased to learn that Mr. Byrd had said the English should do as the Frenchies do, and marry Indians.

The following day we set out for Washington City, the Mandan Chief and Peme were accustomed to houses by now, but they were astonished at the sight of our capitol. They were much taken by the White House, pronounced it a Great Lodge, they wondered did the high rock wall and iron gate mean that our enemies frequently attacked that Lodge.

They spent one entire day watching the workmen placing blocks of stone between the Column heads in the Capitol building, the Mandan Chief thought it would be fine if his People could learn to construct such buildings. Pennsylvania Ave. excited their Admiration much although they were set back by the mud, the Carriages were sunk to the hub. We stayed in a hotel, what impressed Mandan Chief the most was the rosy clusterings of gas lights, which he said turned night into day, he wished much that his People could have such lights. He thought chimneys too a great invention, until it turned cold, then he complained that in eliminating Smoke we also lost the heat, for his part he missed the heat he would put up with the smoke.

On Dec. 30 Capt. Lewis took us to meet Mr. Jefferson at the White House, the President received us warmly, he told me that Capt. Lewis had told him that I had been a valuable man, he wished to express his personal thank you, this set me up considerable.

Mr. Jefferson is much taller than I had supposed, his hair is near as red as that of Capt. C. except that he has streaks of grey, age has however not Bent his Back, he was so straight as a ramrod.

Mr. Jefferson was stiff and pompous in speaking to the Mandan Chief, he was charming and relaxed when he spoke to Peme. She did a courtesy which Mrs. Lewis had taught her, he bent over and took her little hand in his huge one, he bid her welcome to the U. States. His affection for Capt. Lewis and his pride in the Corps of Discovery extended to us all, he said he was most happy to have us in his house.

He is truly a great man, I was excited and embarrassed to meet him, I was afraid I should make a mistake, I can scarce recall how to eat with a knife and fork, I did not know what to say. But he made us all feel welcome, he is easy to talk to, he asked many questions about our voyage, I found I could talk to him as easy as I do to Colter or Drewyer.

He asked were we ever discouraged. Just once, I said, when we were hauling up the river named for him, before I could think what I was saying I blurted out that the Jefferson River was a horrid river.

He laughed, he said he wished that he could see it

some day. I said I should be glad to be his guide, it was a thrill beyond words to be able to speak to the President of the U. States in this manner.

There were many Balls and parties to follow, on the New Year's Day Mr. Jefferson held a grand levee in the White House, on Jan'y 14 there was a gala celebration with the Members of the Congress and Cabinet near 30 toasts were drank. We toasted the People of the U. States, the Constitution, the President, the Congress, Columbus, Capt. Cook & etc.

The final toast as to Capts. Meriwether Lewis and Wm. Clark, by that time I was near too Drunk to stand, but I stood for that one.

Capt. Lewis gave me permission to take Peme and Robin to see my parents, we traveled by stage to Ohio, when we arrived my Father was not at home, my mother gave me a hug, I thought she would never let go, then she hugged Peme and said here was the daughter she had always wanted, there were tears all down her face. When she picked up Robin I thought we should be lucky if we ever got him back. She taught Robin how to say, "Grandma," she fed him candy suckers, he got sick and puked, mother but laughed and cleaned up and gave him some more.

She made a meal for us, it was so grand, better even than the food at the Balls and Banquets we had enjoyed in Washington City. It was exactly what I had dreamed of when I was alone on the prairie, I told her that the thought of her food was what had kept me going, I related how she had appeared to me in the mountains when Colter and I were near to giving up and she urged me to go on, she was overjoyed to hear this, she gave me another hug.

We talked and talked, she had many inquiries, she mostly wanted to know did I get enough to eat, did I catch a cold, & etc.

Jan'y 3, '08.

Peme and Robin and I returned to Washington City in late March of '07. We with the Mandan Chief and his squaw proceeded on to Louisville, where we met Capt. C. or should I write Gen'l C., as he had meanwhile been promoted to the rank of General of the Militia of the Missouri Territory. Capt. Lewis was also promoted, he was now the Governor of Missouri, he stayed in the Capitol for business.

Our party arrived in St. Louis at the commencement of July, Gen'l C. made arrangements for the return of the Mandan Chief to his People. Ensign Pryor commanded the Detachment of Soldiers, there was 13 of us including Gibson, we were joined by a trading party of 32 men, for the most part engagees, Mr. Pierre Chouteau was the leader of this venture. This was sufficient force, according to Gen'l C., to get us past the Sioux and return to the Mandan Chief safely.

Gen'l C. instructed Ensign Pryor to grant me my Discharge at Mandan Village, where I anticipated meeting Colter and setting out immediately for the Yellowstone country, I had resolved after my visit to my parents to never again set foot in civilization.

We proceeded on very well, the engagees put their backs into it, we got past the Sioux country in early September without seeing even one Sioux.

We were thanking God, we were too soon.

At 9 o'clock on the 9th of September we arrived at the lower villages of the Ricaras. The warriors along the bank fired several guns, the shot of which came very near us.

Our interpreter, Mr. Dorion, inquired what they meant, they replied that we should put to shore, that they wished to trade. The Mandan Chief urged Ensign Pryor to ignore those People, but Pryor thought from their former hospitalities to the Corps of Discovery that it should be prudent to show a confidence and he ordered the boats to land.

In a very short time the bank was crowded with 600 or more warriors, there were many Sioux amongst the Ricaras, they were all boiling mad, they were the most of them armed with guns. We were prepared for them, I told Peme to hide below the gunnels. A Mandan woman who was a captive came on the boat, she informed that the Ricaras were at war with the Mandans, they were in an alliance with the Sioux, that they were furious with the Americans for the death of their Chief who had been to Washington City the previous year and died there.

This captive also informed that when Mr. Manual Lisa, a St. Louis trader passed through some weeks before, Drewyer, Collins, and Wiser all being a part of his Party, that the Ricaras had pillaged him of about half of his goods, and suffered him to pass on only when he told them that our party should be expected very soon, that we had the Mandan Chief on board and lots more good than he had, in short he diverted the storm which threatened his own boats by directing the attentions of the Ricaras to ours. The captive said that the Ricaras intended to kill the Mandan Chief and plunder us.

Upon being thus appraised of the blood-thirsty intentions of those Indians, Ensign Pryor had the Mandan Chief secure himself in the cabin, we built a breast work of trunks and boxes and prepared for action, which the Ricaras and Sioux appeared to be putting themselves in readiness to commence. They were checking their bullets and sending away their women and children. I had Peme and Robin secure themselves with the Mandan Chief and looked to my piece.

A Chief of the Ricaras, the Grey Eyes, stepped forward, Pryor greeted him in a friendly fashion.

Pryor suspended a Medal around the neck of the Grey Eyes.

Grey Eyes tore off that Medal and cast it to the ground. Now it starts, I thought.

The Grey Eyes informed us that we should proceed no further, his warriors seized the cable of the barge of Mr. Chouteau which barge contained the merchandise, Grey Eyes said that the soldiers could go on.

Mr. Chouteau begged Pryor not to abandon him in so dangerous a situation.

Make them an offer, Pryor suggested.

Mr. Chouteau then made an offer which ought to have satisfied them, he proposed to leave half of his goods with them.

This did not satisfy, Grey Eyes demanded the whole of the merchandise, some Sioux attempted to carry off the rifles, Mr. Chouteau struck the first of them down with the butt end of his gun.

The Indians then raised a general Whoop, they commenced firing on us while they fell back towards the willows. Two of the engagees were struck.

Fire! roared Pryor, we all fired a well directed volley of Swivels, Blunderbusses and rifles, five or six Indians fell. I had a careful aim, I put my ball though the head of the Grey Eyes. I felt a surge of triumph, I felt an equal surge of horror and shame, this was the first man I ever killed, I watched the blood run down his face I could not take my eyes from him.

The Mandan Chief was chanting his death song, he was greatly afraid, Peme went to comfort him, she was holding Robin by the hand but he shook loose, he was so excited by the fire all around, he stood up to see. I reached for him to pull him down, just as I did a ball struck him full in the belly, the force of that ball threw him from the boat, he was lying in the water, his guts coming from his stomach.

I leaped from the boat to lift him up. Peme was screaming, she leaped too, just as she got to my side to help with Robin a ball struck her between her eyes, the blood spurted from her head like a fountain, it covered my face and chest, I could not see.

I wiped the blood from my eyes, I could see the savage who had shot my wife, he was not 50 yards off on the shore, he was whooping and doing his war dance and shaking his fist at me, I pulled my knife and charged that bastard, he ran toward the willows where the remainder of the Indians were firing their guns.

I caught the murderer before he got half way to the willows, I leaped on his back, I plunged my knife into his heart, the blood pumped out, it was hot and sweet smelling, I was in a frenzy, I could scarcely hold on to my knife, it was slippery from the blood.

I slashed at him with the knife, I cut first above one ear and then the other, I made a slash across his forehead and grabbed his hair and lifted his scalp, I held it high for all those devils to see, at that instant a ball struck me in my thigh and threw me to the ground.

Gibson came running to me, he fired into the willows, then threw his gun down and took hold of me and commenced to drag me back to the boat. I shook him off and attempted to charge those sons of bitches but my leg gave out, I crumbled to the ground, Gibson took me again and pulled me back to the boat, there I passed out.

When I came to it was night, we were paddling so fast as the engagees could paddle down the river, we were in full retreat. The pain in my leg was incredible to describe, the pain in my head was worse. Pryor informed me that the bodies of Peme and Robin had been left behind, that they were dead.

I was still clutching the scalp, I placed it in my pocket.

Where is my knife, I asked, I want my knife. It is gone, Pryor said, lie still, you are bad hurt. I tried to get up, he pushed me back, I pretended to sleep.

When he left me I took a Knife which was at the bottom of the boat, I pulled myself up onto the gunwale and dropped over into the river, I swum ashore and commenced to hobble back to the fight site, I was determined to kill more savages.

I had taken but three steps when I collapsed, I passed out. When I came to I was lying on the bottom of the boat, we were proceeding down the river. I scarcely knew what was happening, I passed out again.

Jan'y 5, '08.

I slept yesterday as a consequence of a dose of landanum from Doctor Farrar, today he wished to give me another dose, I said, No, I am under a compulsion to finish writing this record.

When I next come to we were at the mouth of the Kansas River, we were headed for St. Louis. My pains were intense in the extreme, I had a high fever, gangrene had set in on my leg, Pryor assured me that he should get me back to Fort Belle Fountane and a doctor. That I should be saved.

Do not bother, I said, I wish to die.

I will not let you die, he replied, you are young and have much to live for.

I have nothing to live for, I said, I cannot return to civilization and I cannot live in the Wilderness. I wish to die. I asked him to leave me there at the Kansas, I attempted to get off the boat.

He pushed me back, he said I should be Saved.

The effort of moving sent pains through me such as I never experienced, I puked and passed out again.

When I come to I was in this hospital, Doctor Farrar was beside me, he informed me that he had cut off my leg above the knee, that I was recovering, that I should be well soon.

I wish to die, I said, I have lost my leg, my wife, my son, my chance to live in the Wilderness, I do not wish to live in civilization, I asked him to give me a pistol and leave me alone, he refused.

The following day Gen'l C. came to visit me, he has

come near every day for a month, he talks to me about the future. At first I told him what I had told Pryor and the doctor, that I wished to die.

Inadmissible, he said.

According to Gen'l C. I have a future, he says I can be a successful fur trader, although I want to study to become a lawyer. I have many friends, he says, I am a hero, I have much to live for, I should look to the future, not to the events of the past.

He brings me gossip, he says I shall have a pension of $8 a month from the government, he has, he informs, freed York and given him a six-horse team and a wagon, York is now in the hauling business between Nashville and Richmond, he is the most set up nigger you ever saw, says Gen'l C., he has a bright future, so do you.

Jan'y 6, '08.

I have thought about what Gen'l C. said all night, I have decided that he is right, that life is better than death, that there is much I can still do.

I can do as Gen'l C. suggests and become a lawyer. I would enjoy being a student, reading the works of the great authorities, meeting bright young men, learning the law. I cannot imagine a life more different than the one I have been living since 1803. Sitting and reading rather than moving and doing.

The sedentary life is not what I expected, nor wanted, but it is what I must have, and it does have its appeal. There was a great change in my life when I joined the Corps of Discovery, and I guess it is time for another great change.

I have had enough excitement for one lifetime anyway. I have killed two men, and with all that they was Indians and had started the fight and had killed my wife and son and deserved killing. I don't ever want to kill again. It is wrong. The worst thing is that it is exhilarating, not so much the shooting of Grey Eyes, there was no pleasure in that, but when I plunged my knife into that warrior's heart I felt a rush of pleasure, I was aglow, I was supremely happy, there is no feeling to compare it to.

Well, now I know the answer to the question I asked Rubin Fields, how it felt to kill a man with your hands, and I don't like the answer, I am ashamed of how I felt, I'm glad I will never have to kill again.

Oct. 20, '09.

Once again I thought my journal was complete only to discover that it is not, another entry is a necessity.

In March of 1808 I left St. Louis and proceeded by stage to Lexington, Kentucky, where I took up residence at the University of Transylvania and began my study of law. I found that I enjoyed the work and did well in it, the life of the mind has its own excitements, different from those of the hunter and wanderer to be sure but nevertheless very satisfying. Mr. Noah Webster's dictionary and law books have replaced my rifle and knife as my principle tools. I look forward to hanging out my shingle and participating in Politics. Senator Henry Clay of this city, who has befriended me, urges me to do so.

I have put all thoughts of the Wilderness, of Peme and Robin, and Colter and Drewyer out of my mind. The Expedition seems like a dream to me now.

Or so at least I had thought until today, when Gen'l Clark stopped at my home on his way to Washington and Philadelphia. His wife, former Julia Hancock, is with him, so too is his infant son name Meriwether

Lewis Clark. Gen'l Clark's business in the East is to arrange for the publication of his and Captain Lewis's journals. He informs me that Captain Lewis is very much upset by the announcement that Sgt. Gass will be publishing his journal of the Expedition, this will reduce the market for their journals and give an incomplete account. Gass could not possibly have accurate descriptions of all the new animals and plants we saw, which number in the hundreds, nor can he possibly have accurate maps.

Gen'l C. wished to know, Did I intend on publishing my journal? No, I told him, I do not, my journal was prepared only for myself, and for my children should I ever have any, it is a personal document and contains things I should never want to put before the public.

This pleased the General, he said he was in need of some welcome news, he explained that Governor Lewis has been unwell, he has been drinking and neglecting his affairs, he should have long since arranged for publication of the journals, but has not, now he finds himself beset by his creditors, it appears that the War Department has refused to honor his drafts.

Gen'l Clark explained that Governor Lewis had drawn on the War Department in the Spring of this year for $7,000 in supplies for the St. Louis Missouri Fur Company, organized by Mr. Manual Lisa and charged with returning the Mandan Chief to his village. Mr. Lisa joined forces with all the traders ascending the Missouri and through this show of force was able to get Mandan Chief passed the Sioux and Ricaras and returned him, finally, to his home.

It pleased me much to learn that the Mandan Chief had finally got home, I wish I could be there with him, with Peme and Robin, but it cannot be. Oh how my heart yearns for Peme, I think of her every day.

The War Department refused to honor Governor Lewis's drafts, he was not authorized, the gov't says, to employ private trading companies to do the gov't's business. As a consequence, Governor Lewis is being embarrassed by his creditors, who are calling in the various loans he has taken out. This threatens to leave Governor Lewis in a state of bankruptcy.

This development, Gen'l Clark reported, put Governor Lewis into a depression, his drinking grew worse. At

Gen'l Clark's suggestions, the Governor is now on his way to Washington via the Natchez Trace road, to make his case face-to-face with Sec'y of War Eustis. He also takes with him the journals and his land warrant from the government for 1,600 acres in Missouri. He will place the journals with Mr. Nicholas Biddle of Philadelphia to preparation for publication, and hopes to sell his land warrant.

Gen'l C. says he thinks that things will turn out alright for Governor Lewis, that after all it was the government's responsibility to return Mandan Chief to his village, that Governor Lewis was under direct orders to do so, and that hiring Mr. Lisa for that purpose was the only way to accomplish it.

What concerns him more, he relates, is the fate of the journals. Until Governor Lewis's mind is free of worry he shall not be able to concentrate on the necessary preparations for publication. And until the Journals are published, he concluded, we cannot consider the Expedition to be complete.

We talked far into the night about the members of the Corps of Discovery. Gen'l Clark hears that Colter and Drewyer are doing well in the trapping business on the Yellowstone. Pryor has been promoted to Captain. Rubin Fields joined with Mr. Lisa in the Missouri Fur Company, he helped return the Mandan Chief to his home. Joseph Fields, he sadly reports, has died.

Oct. 21, '09.

This morning at breakfast, the post was delivered, the newspaper from Louisville contained terrible news, it announced that Governor Lewis has died of his own hand at a place called Grinder's Stand on the Natchez Trace.

Gen'l Clark's face went white when he read the news, I thought at first he would pass out, he slumped into a chair, and dropped the newspaper, his head fell forward, he was crushed.

Shortly he got up and began pacing around the table, he could not stop, he was distraught and beside himself.

Finally he stopped and lifted his head and looked at me and exclaimed, I fear O! I fear the weight of his mind has overcome him.

For my part I was in a daze. I could not think, my mind was in a swirl, when Gen'l Clark spoke the horribleness of the thing hit me like a mule kick in the stomach, indeed I had to grab my crutches and go outside to puke, when I came back the General was staring into the ceiling, the tears were rolling down his cheeks, he commenced to shake. I discovered that I was crying too, I had not realized it, I dropped my crutches and began to fall, he took me in his arms, we embraced, our tears mingled, we held each other tight.

We were exhausted, we slumped into our chairs, we poured a glass of whiskey each, we commenced talking.

Gen'l Clark said he had always feared such an outcome, the melancholy ran in Governor Lewis's family, that he blamed the gov't for this, that Governor Lewis was too sensitive, that having his drafts put in question had destroyed his reason.

I said that was perhaps so but that in my mind there is a further reason, it was that Governor Lewis had taken on himself the failure of the Expedition.

What do you mean by failure, Gen'l Clark demanded, he was angry.

I mean, I said, the failure as Governor Lewis saw it. I explained that in my view he blamed himself for all that was unsatisfactory in the outcome. He could not take things as they were, he wanted them to be as President Jefferson wished them to be, when they were not he blamed himself.

He had hoped to bring peace to the tribes along the Missouri and Columbia, that had not happened. They were all at war with one another when we returned.

Capt. Lewis had wished to report that the entire Missouri Valley was fertile and well-watered, that was not the case, much of it is a desert.

Capt. Lewis sought an all-water route from St. Louis to the mouth of the Columbia, with a one- or two-day portage between the rivers, but what he found was the Rocky Mountains, and a two-month portage, and on the other side a Columbia River that could not be navigated. There was no all-water route. That country beyond the Rockies is nearly as remote to us as the moon.

Governor Lewis had wished to discover a tributary of the Missouri coming in from the north from 50 degrees that would establish an American title to the country of the Saskatchewan, that instead on his exploration of the Maria's River he had found that such a river did not exist, that the Maria's barely made 49 degrees.

There was no peace among the Indians, white traders from the U. States can not use the Missouri River because of the Sioux, there were no all-water routes to the Pacific, what Columbus had set out to find was not there, there was no rain nor fertile land on the Missouri beyond Kansas, there was no claim to Saskatchewan.

It distressed Capt. Lewis to report these failures to President Jefferson. He took them on himself, he thought of himself as a failure and worse he thought of the Expedition as a failure.

None of those things was his failure, Gen'l Clark declared, we carried out our orders like soldiers should, we went to the source of the Missouri River as ordered, we made innumerable discoveries of plant and animals previously unknown to science, we prepared maps of what had been a wilderness, we opened the way to the greatest fur country in the world, we were a great success.

No, By God, No, General Clark shouted, we were not failures.

I know that, I said, and you know that, but he did not.

We poured another glass of whiskey, we drank in silence, we were thinking of our friend.

I shall remember him best, said the General, in the summer of 1805, standing at the junction of the Maria's and the Missouri, wondering which was the river for us to follow, examining the beds of the streams, calculating where they came from, observing their velocity and color, and pronouncing the left hand fork was the fork for us. Do you remember, George, he asked.

I remember, I said, we all thought he was wrong, even Cruzzate thought he was wrong.

For myself, Gen'l Clark said almost to himself, I thought that if Capt. Lewis said it was so, then it was so.

We drank again, Gen'l Clark said he remembered too when we had completed the portage of the Great Falls, and we put the skins on Capt. Lewis's boat the Experiment, it was his own invention, he had staked much on it, even his reputation, and she sank.

Do you remember, George, he asked.

She floated like a cork for two hours, I recalled, and then sank like a stone.

Gen'l Clark said at that moment he thought his own heart would sink, he was discouraged in the extreme, he was ready to give up. But Capt. Lewis only shrugged, he lost not a moment's time on regret, he did not curse or rant or rave, he said, Well we must build more canoes, we must get on.

For my part, I said, what I recall best about Capt. Lewis was the night we left the Mandans.

Gen'l C. said he could remember some of it. I have it all in my journal, I said, I took down my journal and read to him:

This little fleet although not quite so respectable as those of Columbus or Capt. Cook, were still viewed by us with as much pleasure as those deservedly famed adventurers ever beheld theirs; and I dare say with quite as much anxiety for their safety and preservation. We are now about to penetrate a country at least two thousand miles in width, on which the foot of civilized man has never trodden; the good or evil it has in store for us is experiment yet to determine, and these little vessels contain every article by which we are to expect to subsist or defend ourselves.

Oh, I cried, I can see him in my mind, sitting by the

fire, wearing moccasins and fringed deer leggings and shirt, his cocked hat set back, his journal on his lap, his face shining with his happiness near as bright as the moon. He was so beautiful.

My voice broke, I commenced to sob.

Go on, Gen'l Clark urged, read more. He poured me another whiskey.

I drank it down and continued: However, entertaining as I do, the most confident hope of succeeding in a voyage which has formed a darling project of mine for the last ten years, I can but esteem this moment of my departure as among the most happy of my life.

I could not go on, I was sobbing.

I am drained of tears, said Gen'l Clark, I can cry no more. Let me read the rest. I handed him my journal:

The Party is in excellent health and spirits, zealously attached to the enterprise, and anxious to proceed; not a whisper or murmur of discontent to be heard among them, but all act in unison, and with the most perfect harmony.

It is too much, said Gen'l Clark, it is more than a man can bear.

He shook himself, he said, George, you must

accompany me to Philadelphia, you will have to interrupt your studies, you shall reside with Mr. Biddle to help him to prepare our journals for publication, you are the only one who can do it, he will have innumerable questions that only you or I can answer and I must attend to my duties in St. Louis.

I protested, I said travel was difficult and painful for me, that I had committed myself to a life of the law. I should have to stay here.

Inadmissible, said Gen'l Clark, you have a duty to Capt. Lewis.

We agreed that in the morning I shall proceed with Gen'l Clark and his family to Philadelphia, I shall assist Mr. Biddle, we shall get the journals published. This in honor of Captain Meriwether Lewis, late commander of the Corps of Discovery and the finest man I ever knew.

Epilogue

THE REUNION

Sept. 24, '36.

Yesterday was the 30th anniversary of the return of the Corps of Discovery to St. Louis. Last evening the young engineering officers who are in charge of the construction of the dykes and levees on the Mississippi River held a dinner at Christy's Inn for Gen'l Clark and myself.

The ghosts were in that room, it was the same room we had held our ball in 30 years ago. These young gentlemen inform us that all the cadets at the Military Academy at West Point read the Journals of Lewis and

Clark, as a consequence they were full of questions. Gen'l Clark, now 66 years of age, was only too happy to answer. Me too, I must confess, as it is flattering in the extreme to have such intelligent young men listen intently to your every word. In addition, the dinner was good, the wine was good, and the cigars and whiskey after dinner were even better.

Gen'l Clark is a bit heavier than I have seen him, his red hair is now grey, his movements slow, but as he talked the years appeared to fall away. His eyes sparkled as I had seen them so often on the journey, as he spoke of our adventures, trials, and dangers, of drudgery and fatigue, of boredom and excitement, of sickness and the death of Sgt. Floyd, of eating horses, dogs and roots, of numbing cold, pelting rain, and baking sun, of rattlesnakes, of buffalo herds that cover the prairie and their faithful shepherds the wolves, of ferocious grizzlies and pesky gnats, of Prickly Pears, of the Sioux and Walla Wallas, of Mandans and Shoshones, Flatheads and Nez Perce, of spectacular mountains, surging rivers, and our first sight of the Pacific Ocean.

Those engineers listened in breathless silence.

For my part, images danced through my mind, of Sacajawea and Charbono and Jean Baptist (whom Gen'l C. persists in calling Pomp) around the fire and the sense they gave us young men of harmony and family and the flow of life. I could see George Drewyer tracking a deer or calling up a turkey. I could hear Capt. C. telling us that we could go on, I could see Capt. Lewis persuading Cameahwait to help us over the mountains. I blinked at the sight of Rubin Fields outracing the fastest Nez Perce. I felt a rush of good feeling when I spotted Colter, when we got back to the tobacco cache on Jefferson River, sitting with his back against a pine, smoking in perfect rapture.

I spoke of these thoughts, Gen'l C. declared that memory was an exquisite thing, that it gave an old man great satisfaction.

The commander of the detachment of officers was a 29-year-old Captain named Robert E. Lee of Virginia. He is the son of Light Horse Harry Lee, the Revolutionary War Hero, and a strikingly handsome young man. The others look up to him as we used to Capts. C. and Lewis. Capt. Lee said he regretted much that he was not born 30 years earlier, that while today all was boredom and routine for an Army officer, in our day all was excitement and discovery. He wished much that he could be part of some great discovery.

You can, Gen'l Clark declared, you can. There is still much to be discovered. Capt. Lee protested that it was not so, Gen'l Clark insisted that it was.

For example, said Gen'l Clark, there is a vast country where the Yellowstone River forms up that has not been seen except by John Colter, and he made no maps nor left any written description.

One of the officers laughed, he said they had all heard of Colter's Hell, a place where there was stink pots and eruptions and bubbling boils of mud, where the rivers ran so hot you could cook a steak in them, where the waterfalls seemed to come straight from heaven itself, where the lakes are without bottom and as blue as the sky. Everyone in the West has heard those stories of Colter's discoveries, he declared, and all knew that they were imagination only.

Gen'l Clark gave the gentleman a long look, and he was about to speak, but I spoke first, I said, Listen you pup, if John Colter said it was so, then it was so.

George is right, Gen'l Clark said, and I hope that some of these days one of you leads an expedition into that country, you will find things exactly as Colter described them.

What happened to Colter, Capt. Lee wished to know. Well, said Gen'l Clark, he stayed in the wilderness for four years, he had adventures of every kind, he was captured by the Blackfeet and escaped from them at precisely that spot that Sacajawea had been captured at Three Forks. He explored the mountain country as no other American ever has. In 1810 he returned to St. Louis with his squaw, he called her Sally, she was a pretty little thing who reminded me of George's squaw Peme. He took up his land warrant and settled on a farm near Daniel Boone at La Charrette.

Gen'l Clark laughed, he said he remembered Colter returning Mr. Boone's knife to him, the one that Mr. Boone had given to me. Mr. Boone was delighted, Gen'l Clark told us, it pleased him to know that his knife had been to the Pacific Ocean and back and had done good service.

After all Colter's adventures and dangers, Gen'l C. continued, it was damnable that a fever came and took him off in 1813.

I proposed a toast to John Colter, he was the first mountain man, I said, and the best of them all. I drank to that.

What about Drewyer, one of the officers asked. He was the greatest hunter of our nation's history, I said. Gen'l Clark reported that Colter had told him that Drewyer had been killed by the Blackfeet at Three Forks in 1810.

I would like to know, I said, how many Blackfeet he got first.

We talked of the others. Pryor died five years ago in the Indian Territory of Oklahoma, where he was an agent for the Osage Indians and had a squaw for a wife. Sgt. Gass lost an eye in the late war with Britain, he is now farming in Ohio.

And what of your interpreter and his squaw, Capt. Lee inquired.

Yes, all the officers pitched in, tell us about your famous Indian guide.

She Was Not Our Guide, Gen'l Clark thundered. He pounded his fist down on the table and knocked over whiskey glasses.

She Was Not Our Guide! She was the squaw of our interpreter only.

Well, Gen'l, I said so softly as I could, I can see her now, standing on the cliff over Three Forks, Pomp strapped to her back, pointing her finger East, to the gap in the mountains that we should take to get to the Yellowstone. She certainly looked like a guide to me then.

Well, he sputtered and squirmed a bit, and poured another whiskey all around, he hemmed and hawed, and finally allowed as how that was true.

But By God! he said, It is not true what people say, that Sacajawea was our guide to the Pacific Ocean. It makes my blood boil, he said, to think that people could suppose that a child—and a girl at that—was the guide for the Lewis and Clark Expedition.

He sipped his whiskey, we were all silent, the red came off his face, he gave a sigh and another and then a smile came to him.

You know, boys, he said, she was a damn fine woman. By God, I have never said this to anyone, I never even knew it until now.

He hiccupped, he allowed as how he was not accustomed to so much drink, but he reminded himself that this was a very special occasion, and he took another sip.

Well, he said, if old Charbono would have died on the expedition, I'd have been tempted to do as George and Colter and so many of the men did, and take a squaw for a wife.

He was embarrassed by the thought but still eager to talk about Sacajawea, so he went on.

Do you remember, George, he asked me, the time the canoe broadsided to the wind and filled, due entirely to Charbono's negligence, and Sacajawea held her seat in the stern and picked up all these floating articles, some of our most valuable instruments, parts of the journals themselves, all would have been lost but for her. She sat there in that stern, just as calm as could be while Charbono cried out to His God for Mercy, Cruzzate in the bow was threatening to shoot Charbono if he did not take up the tiller and do his duty, the canoe awash and near sinking, Sacajawea sat there with her cradleboard and baby, just saving the whole Expedition.

I remember, I said, and do you remember the number of times she found us roots when we would have otherwise fasted?

You always think of your stomach first, Gen'l Clark laughed, I think of how many times her presence saved us fights with the Indians, they knew we were not a war party thanks to her presence.

But what he thought of even more, Gen'l C. said, was her service as an interpreter. He thought she was the only we should have paid, she did more than old Charbono. He recalled meeting with Cameahwait, that was another time she saved the Expedition.

I said that I could recall her smile, her giggle, her laugh, I remembered how nice she was just to look at, I recalled her confidence in us, no matter how bad things looked she was always sure we could get through, she gave us joy and laughs and confidence in ourselves.

Gen'l Clark proposed a toast to Sacajawea. "To the interpreter's squaw. She was not our guide to the Pacific

Ocean, but we should never have got there or back, without her.

We drank and gave three cheers for Sacajawea.

So what happened to her, Capt. Lee was insistent on knowing.

Gen'l Clark said she and Charbono came down with Colter in 1810. They stayed in St. Louis over the winter. Sacajawea could not warm to the city, Charbono would have stayed but she was determined on going back to Mandan Village, which they did in the Spring. She died of a fever the next Spring, one year after Colter, both of them still very young.

Capt. Lee wished to know what happened to her son.

Gen'l Clark's face filled with pleasure, he said, My Boy Pomp has made me as proud of him as I am of my boy George here. Pomp, he said, stayed in St. Louis with him, he sent Pomp to the Jesuits for an education, on Sundays he and Pomp would go hunting together. He spent his summer with the Mandans, the rest of the year in St. Louis.

When Baptist, as all but Gen'l C. called him, was 20

years old, a German prince came to St. Louis for an expedition up the Missouri. He wanted a guide, Gen'l C. recommended Baptist, the expedition was a success, the Prince asked Baptist to come to Germany, which he did.

Baptist was a sensation in Europe, he was the guest of honor at fetes and balls and etc. in castles and palaces. I thought to myself as Gen'l C. talked that if ever there was a person born to travel and see new and strange sights, it was Jean Baptist Charbono.

Gen'l C. reported that Baptist came back to St. Louis six years ago, he said that he had had enough of civilization, that it was back to the Indians for him. Since then he has been a mountain man, he earns money from time to time by serving as a guide and interpreter for Army explorers.

By God, what an interpreter he must be, Gen'l Clark declared. He asked us to think of it, the boy speaks English, German, French and Spanish, he knows Mandan and Minnitaree, Shoshone and Sioux, Cheyenne and Nez Perce, and who knows what else, plus the sign language.

Let's drink to Baptist, I proposed, I had a picture in my

mind of a big-eyed infant staring out of his cradleboard, laughing and laughing as we descended the rapids of the Columbia. I confess it sets me back some to think of Pomp as a 31-year-old man who is equally at home in European courts and the American wilderness.

Sept. 27, '36.

Capt. Lee came to visit me yesterday, he said he wished to hear of the lessons I had learned on the Expedition. I could not think of why he asked me such a question, he informed me that he had always thought of Lewis and Clark as the perfect officers, that he was sure they had lessons to teach him, that he was looking for ways to improve himself as an officer, and that thus if he could find out what I had learned he could have some insight into the methods of Lewis and Clark.

Well, I said, that is all rather grand and sweeping, and I am preparing a case, and I have never thought of such a question, I have no answer.

Well, think about it now, he urged, and tell me. Which I did, as follows.

I learned the importance of team work, I said, of all

joining together to work to achieve something, of each man feeling confidence in all of the others, and of all to have confidence in one. The reason for the failure of Ensign Pryor's Expedition is that we were not a team. The engagees went one way, the soldiers went the other, and the soldiers were not together for long enough to become a team.

I said I thought that had Drewyer and Colter and the Capts. been there I should still have my wife, my son and my leg.

I had also learned the importance of leadership, of having leaders you can trust. No great Enterprise can succeed without great leaders and we need them.

I learned, I said, never to give up, even when you are lost without your balls.

I learned patience. That was a lesson Drewyer taught me. It has helped me much as a lawyer and politician.

Since the Expedition I have learned another lesson, I said, it is to have faith in progress, to believe that whatever the difficulty, the inventiveness of man can overcome it. Just to think of what has happened since our Expedition, in just thirty years. Steamboats ply all our rivers, why you can go from St. Louis to Mandan Village and beyond without once touching a paddle or pole or cord.

And now the railroads, they are the wonder of all time, they make the 19th Century the most exciting century of all to live in, they give us and our country unlimited horizons.

I said I had rode the Baltimore and the Ohio from Harper's Ferry to Washington City last year, we went nearly 30 miles an hour, why when they get the track laid we shall be getting from here to Washington City in one day.

You can have no idea, Capt. Lee, I said, what an impression that makes on the mind of a man who once thought covering 80 miles in a day was near flying.

I said I learned never to judge a people until I had lived among them, that when I hear my planter friends curse the Negro race I think of York, as fine a man as there was among us, and I know there is something wrong with their system of slavery, the fault lies not in the Negro race.

When I hear the whites call Indians savages, I who of

all people have a right to believe that, think instead of Sacajawea and Peme and the Mandan Chief and Eagle and Little Hawk, and Cameahwait, and Old Toby, and I think what fools these whites are.

When I hear whites damn all half-breeds as lazy and incompetent and the worst of both races I think of Cruzzate and Drewyer and Pomp and Robin and Charbono, and I remind myself that this is only ignorance talking.

Capt. Lee wished to know, was it true that I carried an Indian scalp in my pocket always.

It is not, I laughed, but I carry a handkerchief and let people say what they will. Recall that I am a politician; it serves me well to have people point and whisper that there is the scalp of the Indian Mr. Shannon killed with a knife to the heart, he lifted the scalp himself. I never have to mention it, just the bulge in my pocket reminds people of who I am.

But, I confessed, I was planning to use that scalp to get a murderous criminal hanged, I explained that in two days I will begin prosecuting a murder case. The accused, a man named Hibbs, has killed an Indian woman. His defense is simple, that she was only a squaw.

Now, I said, I am going after this monster. He is an evil-spirited man of great cruelty, he enjoys slashing and beating on Indian women, this is by no means the first he has killed.

So when I am doing my summation, I'll wave the scalp. I'll be quite a sight on my crutches, I'll have the jury's attention for real.

And I'll tell that jury that Hibbs deserves to be hanged just as bad as this Indian whose scalp I hold here deserved to be killed, that their crimes are equal, and in fact extremely the same.

I was worked up, I was shouting at the end, Capt. Lee brought me a glass of water and said he thought that ought to move the jury. But watch your temper, Capt. Lee said, you are getting a little old to be getting so worked up.

I returned to the subject of lessons. I said I had learned not just a tolerance of differences, but the strength and greatness of differences. I learned that there is much to learn from all, whatever their situation.

We of the Corps of Discovery came from all over the world, white men from Europe and America, a red woman and her son from the Missouri River, half breeds from Canada, a black man from Africa, all was essential to the success of our Enterprise.

So it seems to me to be the case with our great country, I said, its greatness comes from the diversity of people, all making their own contributions.

But the greatest lesson of all, I told Capt. Lee, was that when you just can't go on, you can. It is a lesson that served me in good stead when I lost my leg. I learned the importance of setting a goal, whether it be getting to the Pacific Ocean, or becoming a one-legged lawyer, and staying with it, no matter the obstacles.

I regret though, most that I lost Peme. I never loved another woman, I never knew such joy as when I slept with her. She was as beautiful as a new-born fawn, she would have grown into a fine woman, she was a good mother, she could laugh and joke, everything about her was honest and open and lovely, I loved her much.

But still I know that her death was to my benefit, that I am better satisfied with life in civilization than I could have been with life in the wilderness.

A wilderness life is a selfish life, the mountain man lives for himself alone. That is to say he indulges and does not give. There is much to be said for indulgence, the wild life brings many wonderful pleasures. But indulgence cannot be so satisfactory as service to others. It is in civilization that we can make a contribution to improving the lot of our fellow man, and that feeling of having served others is the best feeling of all.

The rejection of civilization for the wilderness is a rejection of people. The mountain man has no friends, beyond a partner and his squaw. I don't think I could live without friends, further, I like people, I like to be around them, hear them talk, exchange information and ideas and gossip. We had all that on the Corps of Discovery, Colter and I never could have had it by ourselves.

There is another reason I am glad I chose civilization. To live in the wild, you must be ready to kill, or be killed. The wild life is a violent life, death lurks around every tree trunk. Colter killed plenty of Indians, so did Drewyer, before the Indians got Drewyer and damn near got Colter. I do not know which I would have feared the most, the enjoyment of killing or the constant threat of death.

But although I am glad I was not there, I still envy Colter and Drewyer those years in the wilderness, when it was truly a wilderness, the best hunting, as Drewyer said, any human being ever saw.

Well, it was not to be, and what I have is satisfying to me. I shall go back to preparing my case, pleased with myself and what I have done with my life.

St. Louis Post
September 30, 1836

George Shannon, Esq., died yesterday. He was 50 years old.

Born in Pennsylvania, Mr. Shannon was the youngest member of the Lewis and Clark Expedition. After losing his leg in an Indian fight, he became a lawyer. He was Mr. Nicholas Biddle's assistant in the preparation of the Journals of Lewis and Clark for publication. He practiced law in Lexington, Kentucky, where he was a member of the State Legislature from 1820 to 1824. He was a leading Whig in the state and a close associate for Senator Henry Clay. In 1825 he moved to St. Charles, Missouri, where he practiced law and served two terms as State Senator. Since 1833 he has been the U.S. attorney for Missouri.

Mr. Shannon collapsed in a courtroom while prosecuting a murder case. The funeral will be on Monday, with General William Clark delivering the eulogy.

EDITOR'S NOTE

George Shannon, the triumphant young narrator of this journal, was only a teenager and the youngest member of the Corps of Discovery in 1803. During the epoch-making journey he might have kept a journal quite similar to this one. Or he might have been too exhilarated *having* adventures in the wilderness to actually write them down. We may never know. And yet the pages of this journal illuminate an entire generation's fears and dreams, spirit, and vision as they pioneered the way West. So while the language and spelling in this journal are not at all modern and occasionally might seem puzzling or even incorrect, this is indeed deliberate. There is no better way to discover the flavor of an era now gone.